I0667894

Invisible Girlfriend

love, life and beyond

About the Author

Ekta Renu Chandna acquired her post-graduate degree in Marketing from Bharati Vidyapeeth University (Delhi). She lives with her parents in Delhi. She is a day-dreamer and has a habit of conjuring up stories in her mind. This is her debut book, inspired by her dream.

Visit www.ektachandna.com to know more about the author and her work.

Invisible Girlfriend

love, life and beyond

Ekta Renu Chandna

ZORBA BOOKS

ZORBA BOOKS

Published in India by Zorba Books, 2018

Website: www.zorbabooks.com
Email: info@zorbabooks.com

Copyright © Ekta Chandna

ISBN Print Book - 978-93-87456-27-3
ISBN eBook - 978-93-87456-28-0

All rights reserved. No part of this book may be reproduced or transmitted in any form or by any means, electronic or mechanical, including photocopying, recording, or by an information storage and retrieval system—except by a reviewer who may quote brief passages in a review to be printed in a magazine, newspaper, or on the Web—without permission in writing from the copyright owner.

Although the author and publisher have made every effort to ensure the accuracy and completeness of information contained in this book, we assume no responsibility for errors, inaccuracies, omissions, or any inconsistencies herein. Any slights on people, places, or organizations are unintentional.

Zorba Books Pvt. Ltd.(opc)
Gurgaon, INDIA

Printed at Repro Knowledgecast Limited, Thane

Dedication

To my mother, Renu Chandna—who always supports
and motivates me to follow my dream of writing.

Acknowledgment

A huge thanks to—

God, for the words.

My parents, Dalip Chandna and Renu Chandna,
for their unconditional love and support,
for letting me follow my dreams.

My ever-supporting sister, Nikita.

The Publishing Team at Zorba Books.

Contents

I was a happy boy, until the day my girlfriend became invisible. Yes! She really became invisible.

Hello, I am Sid, and this is my story.

Chapter 1
First Sight

"*S*id, Wake up! You are going to be late for school," Mom announced.

"I don't want to go to school," I said meekly while covering my head with a bed-sheet. Mom pulled away the bedsheet.

"Why?" Mom asked with a raised eyebrow.

"I am tired," I lied.

"Sid, you can't lie to me. You are not tired."

"How do you know, Mom?"

"I am your mom. I know when you lie," she said confidently.

"Mom, please I don't want to go to school today."

"Siddharth Ahuja, you are seventeen years old, but sometimes you act like a five-year-old. Don't make excuses, get ready, and come downstairs," Mom said while opening the window of my room.

"Mom, please call me Sid. The name 'Siddharth' is so old-fashioned."

"Okay, but hurry up."

I went to my bathroom and got ready in minimal time. I wore my favourite black jeans and a brown hoodie. I brushed my hair quickly and fixed it with gel. I took off my phone from the charger, slung my bag over my right shoulder and went downstairs.

My parents were sitting in the garden area. Dad was reading the newspaper and Mom was talking on the phone with her patient. I was the only child of my parents. I lived in Mussoorie, a beautiful hill station in India, with my parents. I had everything one could ask for—caring parents, a big beautiful house, and loyal friends. My parents were doctors by profession, and they had quite an excellent reputation in the town since they owned a big hospital which was one of the leading medical institutions in Mussoorie.

Rita, our house-help, served me an omelette with brown bread and poured orange juice into my glass. Rita was of average height, had chubby cheeks and brown hair. She had been working at my home for the past ten years. She was in her mid-forties now. She was like a family member to us and always made delicious breakfast for me. I swiftly finished my meal.

"Sid, your driver is on holiday today, and we are getting late for the hospital. So, you have to go to school on your own," Dad said.

I knew how to drive, but my parents did not give me permission to drive the car until I turned eighteen. So, I decided to walk. After all, my college was just twenty minutes away from my home.

I was walking as fast as I could. The weather was cold, and a strong breeze was constantly blowing. Suddenly, I saw an exceptionally beautiful girl walking down the street. She looked stunning in black jeans and a pink t-shirt. She looked like an angel. I instantly felt a strong connection with her.

She had eyes of a colour unknown to me while her hair was brown and tied in a ponytail. Her pink lipstick perfectly matched her fair skin tone. Words failed to describe her. A girl like her was hard to forget, and that is why I could not get her out of my mind since the moment I saw her for the first time. I was so spellbound by her beauty that I started following her.

"Sid! Sid!" I heard a familiar voice calling me.

I turned towards the voice, "John . . . "

John and I had been best friends since our childhood. He was a tall, dark and handsome boy with black hair and was the captain of the basketball team and an excellent student. Moreover, he was also the best-dressed boy of our college.

"Yes, it's me, my friend. Where are you going?" John asked while putting his phone in the pocket of his jeans.

"What are *you* doing here?" I asked.

"I saw you from afar. So, I came here to meet you."

I turned back to look at that girl again, but she had disappeared. "Oh no! I lost her," I muttered under my breathe.

"What?"

"It's nothing."

"Hurry up. We are getting late. We have to catch the History class on time," John prompted.

"Oh! Yes. How can I forget?"

I rushed towards my school with John. I never liked my History class because of my History teacher Mr. Roy.

He always annoyed me, and it seemed to me it was on purpose. As usual, I was not interested in attending his class, but I had to because of my parents. When I reached the class, I straight away went to my seat because I did not want Mr. Roy to scold me again as I was late, but luckily, he was not there.

I was looking out of the window and thinking about the girl I had seen in the morning when Mr. Roy arrived in the classroom, but I was not paying attention. Suddenly, I heard a very sweet voice, and I looked up to see a baby-faced girl enter the classroom. It was the same girl I had seen in the morning on the street!

Mr. Roy asked her to introduce herself, and I thanked God for sending her to my class.

"Hey everyone! I am Angel Jaswal, but you can call me AJ. I just moved here with my family. My favourite subject is History," she introduced herself. She seemed very innocent and soft-spoken.

Mr. Roy told her to take a seat. Luckily, she came and sat next to me! My heartbeat increased suddenly. I was feeling incredibly nervous, but somehow, I managed to say: "Hey, I am Sid."

"Hey," she replied.

Mr. Roy started his boring lecture, but I was staring transfixed only at her and admiring her flawless skin. I could not focus on anything else during the entire lecture except her. She, on the other hand, was so absorbed in the lecture that she did not seem to notice me gawking at her. As I moved my gaze away from her, I saw Mr. Roy staring angrily at me.

At that moment, the bell rang loudly making me jump; AJ was out of her seat instantly. When I came out of the classroom, AJ was not there. Then I thought I would catch her in the English class, which was my favourite class, but she was not there either.

Just then, I saw Nikita in the hallway. Nikita was the most popular girl in our school whom everybody wanted to befriend. She was of average height, skinny built, and fair complexion. She was my best friend John's girlfriend, but she did not like me much. I thought of asking her about AJ. She was chatting with two other girls. Of the two girls, one was tall, skinny, with straight hair, while another was short, heavy-built, with an untidy ponytail.

"Hey, Nikita, have you seen that new girl AJ?"

"Yes," she replied.

"That's good. Do you know where she is?" I asked politely.

"She left early from school," she said. "Her parents came to pick her up."

"But, why did she leave early? Any idea, Nikita?"

"No, but if that matters to you that much, you can ask her yourself tomorrow," she said rudely.

I expressed my gratitude to her even though she was rude to me. I left the college in the hope of seeing AJ again the next morning. I went to the parking area of my school. My driver was waiting for me there. I sat inside the car, and we left for my home.

Chapter 2

Excitement

"*S*id, wake up, it's 6.30 in the morning, and you are still in the bed," Mom yelled from downstairs.

"I am not in bed," I said while coming downstairs. "Good morning, my beautiful mom."

"Am I dreaming?"

"No! Mom, I woke up at 5.45 a.m."

"Are you all right?"

"Yes, Mom," I said while giving her a kiss on her cheek. "Mom, what are we having for breakfast?"

"Omellete, bread and orange juice," she said.

"Yummy, My favourite breakfast."

I went to the garden area where my father was reading the newspaper. He liked to read the newspaper before breakfast. He was very specific about his routine and quite relished it.

"Good morning, son," my father said while folding the newspaper.

"Good morning."

Rita served us the breakfast. I hurriedly finished my breakfast, taking such big bites that I must have looked like a buffoon to my parents. I wanted to go to school as soon as possible. I wanted to see AJ again. I was not able to sleep a wink the whole night because of her; I felt so restless and excited at the thought of seeing AJ the next day. Though I never believed in love at first sight, I fell for her the very movement I laid eyes on her.

"Why are you in such a hurry?" My father questioned.

"I don't want to be late for my History class."

"But you hate History, right? my mom asked, with one eyebrow raised.

"Not anymore," I lied.

"You know you can't lie to me. So, why do you even try?"

"Oh, Mom! I am getting late. I will tell you later." I ran to the parking area. My driver was waiting for me in our white Mercedes. I was brimming with excitement because I would finally meet AJ now, after a long night's wait. When I reached the school, I stepped out of my car in a hurry. I was going to the History class. Suddenly, John appeared in front of me and stopped me in my tracks.

"Hey, Sid!" he said.

"Hey, John, what happened?" I replied absent-mindedly. I was in a hurry.

"What happened to you? Why are you in such a hurry?"

"I don't want to be late for the History class."

"Oh, really? Since when did you start liking the History class?" he asked with a raised eyebrow.

"I *don't* like it. I just don't want to be late for it," I said. I was getting desperate with every minute passing. I wanted to see AJ!

"What?"

"Nothing. You tell me, why did you stop me? Is it something urgent?" I changed the topic.

"I have two tickets for the music concert happening in our town in the evening."

"No, I don't want to go." I did not like to go to the crowded places.

"Oh! But why? Our favourite rock band is coming."

"I have to go to my grandparents' house in the evening."

Suddenly, the bell rang, and both of us went to the class. The moment I entered, my eyes started searching for AJ, and then I finally saw her! She was sitting next to my seat. She was wearing a black dress with high black heels, and her brown hair was tied in a high ponytail. She looked stunning.

"Hey, AJ!" I greeted her.

"Hey, Sid," she replied.

"You remember my name?"

"Of course, I do," she said.

I was delighted because she remembered my name. I was on the top of the world! Just then, Mr. Roy arrived in the class. During the whole lecture, I was looking only at AJ. Her hair had come loose from the confines of the ponytail and had cascaded over her shoulder, and her face was emanating a radiant glow. This time she noticed that I was watching her, but she did not say anything. At that moment, the bell rang loudly. As we were about to leave, Mr. Roy caught hold of me and started scolding me about my lack of attentiveness in the class. Even as he talked, my eyes were fixed on AJ who was packing her bag.

"Sir, it's my free period. Can I go now?"

"Yes, you can. . . but start paying attention in the class or else you will not achieve anything in your life," he said with finality. He looked seriously annoyed. I paid him no attention.

AJ was just about to leave the class. I caught up with her and gathered all of my courage and asked her, "Hey AJ, will you have lunch with me in the cafeteria?"

She hesitated a bit, but then replied politely, "Yes, of course."

"Okay, then let's go to the cafeteria together." I was overjoyed.

The cafeteria was the place I liked the most in my school. AJ and I walked to the cafeteria together. AJ was wearing high heels, but she was still shorter than me. Like all the men in my family, I was quite tall.

I grabbed two burgers and two cans of soda. The cafeteria was full, but fortunately, I found some empty seating space at one corner of the cafeteria, and we both went and sat there with the food. I was feeling blissful, and my heart was pounding hard at my chest, and I was not able to believe that I was actually having lunch with AJ. AJ, on the other hand, was sitting silently.

"So, AJ, do you like our school?" I asked.

"Yes, very much," she replied.

"But I need to catch up on the English class that I missed yesterday. Will you give me your English class notes?" she asked me politely.

"Yes, of course. Why not?" I replied merrily.

We sat there for one whole hour. We talked to each other about school and our family backgrounds. She seemed a little dejected while she was talking about her family, I noticed. She told me her father was an engineer and her mother was a homemaker; she also had a younger brother. I also told her about my parents. We both kept talking to each other about all things under the sun.

I soon realized that AJ was not like other girls. She was quiet, calm, and there was something mysterious about her. I could not place my finger on it, though. I was so immersed in talking to her that I did not notice that everybody was staring at us. I thought both of us looked great together and that is why everybody was staring like that. AJ's food tray was lying untouched. She had not even opened her can of soda.

"Why are you not eating your lunch?" I inquired.

"I am not hungry."

"So, what do you like besides the History class? I mean, what are your hobbies?"

"I like playing basketball."

"Really? That's my favourite game, and I am also the Vice Captain of our school basketball team."

"Oh, that's good. That's why you look so fit."

I could not help but blush at her comment. I was so nervous, but I did not let it show on my face.

"I also love to listen to romantic Hindi songs," AJ said.

"Me too! Oh my God! Our choices are so similar."

"Do you like reading also?" I asked.

"Oh, yes. Although romance novels are my favourite."

I beamed with happiness on hearing that. "I also love to read romantic novels," I said.

Eventually, I found that AJ and I had lots of things in common. I was feeling a strong connection with her already. A strange affinity which I could not really explain.

It was time to go to our next class now that the lunch break was over. AJ sat next to me as usual. The English class was my favourite, but I was not able to pay attention because of AJ's presence so close to me. I was feeling transported to some other world altogether.

"Sid! Sid!" I could vaguely hear a male voice coming from afar.

I shook my head to jolt me back to reality. "Yes, sir!"

"Where are you lost?" All the students started laughing.

"Sorry, sir."

"It's okay, but please pay attention now."

"Yes, sir."

After school, AJ and I walked to the parking area. My driver was waiting for me there. The weather was getting cold and chilly. I took out a black jacket from my bag and wore it.

"AJ, can I drop you somewhere?"

"Oh! No! No!" She looked shocked at the mere thought of me dropping her home. So, I did not insist.

"Okay, as you say." I did not want to make her uncomfortable.

I sat in my car and rolled down the window to wave goodbye to AJ. As the driver started the car, I turned to take one last look at AJ, but to my surprise, she was not there. It was as if she had disappeared like smoke in the air.

Chapter 3

Love Confession

*A*s I opened my eyes the next morning, I felt like something had changed inside me. I jumped out of bed and went to the bathroom. I splashed some water on my face and went back to my room where the sunlight was streaming inside through the window. I looked out of the window and found that it was a pleasant and sunny day. Then, I noticed that someone was standing below the tree just outside my house. As I paid close attention, I realized to my utter shock that it was none other than AJ!

I was astonished and happy to see her there. I ran downstairs and flung the gates open to go outside. But till the time I reached there, she was gone. I made my way back to my house, dejected. I was very perturbed. I did not know why she came and then left without meeting me. It was a very unsettling experience. I do not know why, but I was suspicious that something was not right.

"Sid!" Rita emerged from the dining room.

"Yes, Rita."

"Your parents have left early today. They had an urgent meeting at the hospital."

"Oh! Okay."

"So, what do you want to eat?" Rita asked politely.

"I want a bowl of cereal and a glass of orange juice."

"Okay, sure." Rita said and went to the kitchen.

My phone rang loudly. My friend John was calling. I was not in the mood to talk to him, but I answered the phone anyway.

"Hey, Sid. What's your plan for today?"

"Plan for what? Don't you want to go to school today?"

"It's Sunday, you idiot! Who goes to school on a Sunday?" John laughed.

I got so lost in my thoughts about the incident that had just transpired that I totally forgot that it was Sunday. John and Nikita were going to the mall for bowling. I did not want to go anywhere. I just wanted to sit and laze around at home.

"I am not well," I lied.

"Oh, in that case, you should take rest. See you at school tomorrow then." I hung up the phone.

Rita served me the breakfast. After finishing my meal, I went to my room and let my mind wander. *Why did she come? Why did she leave without meeting me?* I wanted to meet her, but I did not know where she lived. The rest of my day went in obsessing over my thoughts.

In the evening, when my parents came back from the hospital, we all went outside for dinner in my dad's black BMW. When we reached the restaurant, it was virtually empty. The ambiance of the restaurant was quiet and classy. The background music was soft and peaceful. It was one of the most famous restaurants in the town. We usually go there on Sundays. We all got seated at our usual table near the window. My mom excused herself to go to the restroom. I got lost in my thoughts once again.

"Sid, why do you seem so lost?" Dad asked. I shook my head in denial.

"Nothing, Dad. I just have a headache. Don't tell this to Mom though. She worries too much."

"Okay, I will not, but here, take this tablet." My dad handed me a painkiller that he pulled out from his bag.

Mom came back from the restroom. A tall, skinny tired-looking boy appeared in front of us with a menu card to take our orders. The designer silver glasses and plates placed on the table in front of us looked extravagant.

"What will you like to order?" he asked.

"I will have a Chinese platter and a diet soda," I replied.

Mom and Dad also ordered for themselves. After about twenty minutes, the waiter appeared with our order and also served the same on to our expensive plates. The Chinese platter which came on a hot sizzler plate looked very appetizing. After finishing the lovely meal, we went to an ice-cream parlour.

"What will you have, sir?" the lady at the counter asked my dad.

I ordered a chocolate ice-cream sundae, and my parents ordered a mango sundae. After finishing up, our driver who was waiting for us in the parking area drove us back home.

Next day I got up very early. I took a long relaxing bath and went downstairs after dressing up. After having breakfast with my parents, I left for school. As I reached the parking area, I spotted AJ. I thought of probing her about yesterday's incident.

"Hi Sid, how are you?" she said graciously.

"I am fine. How are you? How did you spend your weekend?" I asked with curiosity.

"I went out of town with my parents and brother for a picnic."

"What! But . . . I don't understand . . . I . . . I saw you outside my house on Sunday!"

"No, that cannot be! You must have seen somebody else.".

"Hmm. . . Maybe." I mumbled, unconvinced.

"Should we go to the class?" AJ asked politely.

As we walked to the class, I kept replaying the incident in my mind. I was sure that I saw AJ in the morning, but then, I figured why would she lie to me? There was a possibility that I had seen somebody else. AJ was looking at me quietly all this while.

"AJ, could you please give me your mobile number?" I asked cordially.

"Err. . . I don't have a phone, sorry," AJ replied.

"Oh, No problem. Give me your landline number in that case."

"Sorry, I can't. My parents are very strict. They do not allow me to talk on the phone with boys." She seemed uncomfortable.

"Oh." I did not want to make her more uncomfortable. So, I changed the topic.

"Have you done your homework?"

"Yes, have you?"

"Nope, I don't like History at all. It's the worst subject. Whenever I open the History book, I feel either sick or sleepy."

AJ sputtered out a laugh.

As the days went by, we became close to each other. We used to go everywhere together—the classes, the cafeteria, etc. Our bond was growing stronger.

One day, she was sitting in the classroom all alone. Hardly anyone had come to the school that day because of the heavy rain. She was wearing a simple pink t-shirt and blue jeans, yet she looked so beautiful. She was looking out of the window and seemed to be gloomy and desolate.

"Hey, AJ. How are you today?" I asked, politely.

"Hey, I am fine. How are you?" AJ asked, graciously.

"I am fine," I replied.

"Sid, I want to tell you something about me."

"Is that so? But AJ, if you don't mind, I want to confess something first," I said cautiously.

"Sid, listen to me first."

"No, please let me speak first, or I would not be able to speak later."

"Alright. What do you want to confess, Sid?"

My heart was pounding, and I had sweat all over my body, but still, I gathered all my courage, and I said, "AJ, I love you."

Suddenly, Mr. Roy entered the classroom with some other students. Everybody started to stare at me like I was an idiot and started mumbling and giggling among themselves. I did not understand why they were making fun of me like that. Perhaps they had heard my confession of love to AJ. It was a very awkward moment for both of us.

Mr. Roy started his lecture, and I kept thinking about how AJ would respond to my declaration of love. She was sitting right next to me, but she was avoiding eye contact with me. I tried to talk to her after the class, but she totally ignored me.

I felt awful. In the free period, I went to the library. I saw AJ there. She was sitting alone at a corner table, reading. I waved to her, but she did not see me. I was waving my hand like mad, but she never once looked in my direction. I felt it was deliberate. It broke my heart, and I headed back home feeling despondent.

Chapter 4

Awkward Silence

"*W*elcome home, son," my mom said. She was beaming.

"Good evening, Mom."

She was saying something to me, but I did not pay any attention. I straight away went to my room. I threw my bag on the couch, took off my shoes and threw them in the corner. I wore my pajamas with a white t-shirt, and I lay down on my bed and did not realize when I passed out. In the evening, Rita came to my room with dinner.

"Where is Mom, Rita?" I was feeling dreadful because I did not listen to her when she was saying something to me in the afternoon.

"She went to the hospital. Your father had called her in the evening from there, and she told me that they would come late at night."

"Oh."

"Do you need anything else?" she asked while serving me the dinner."

"Please, get me a cup of coffee."

"Okay, right away." She closed the door while going out.

I ate the dinner alone. Rita brought a cup of coffee in my favourite black ceramic mug, and after cleaning my bed, she left. At night, I was lying on my bed thinking about AJ. *What have I done? Why did I confess my feelings for her? I should have waited for some more days.* I kept tossing and turning in my bed. I felt awful. I got up and drank a glass of water. I switched on the television to distract myself from my thoughts, but it did not help.

The next day, I apologized to my mother for my bad behaviour. She forgave me instantly. After eating breakfast, my driver dropped me at school. I saw AJ in the hallway in school on my way to the classroom, but she did not even notice me. She was totally ignoring me as if I was invisible! That really hurt me a lot.

Some more days passed in this manner; she did not talk to me at all, she was still totally ignoring me. I was distraught. Then one day, I saw her in the cafeteria. She was sitting alone in the corner like she always did. The whole cafeteria was empty because of the music competition going on in the school basement. I thought this was the right time to talk to her.

"Hey, AJ," I said, as I sat on the chair.

"Hey, Sid," she said in a fragile voice.

"Why are you ignoring me, AJ? What is the matter?" I asked her somewhat meekly.

"No . . . I am not," she replied, without making any eye contact.

"But you have been ignoring me since the day I confessed my feelings for you."

"No, I am not ignoring you. Actually, I did not have the courage to talk to you." Her tone was weak.

"Courage? But for what?" I asked her, surprised.

"I didn't have the courage to accept my feelings for you," she replied.

For a minute, I was stunned into silence. I could not believe my ears! I was ecstatic and so relieved but also a bit frustrated because I had been silently suffering for so many days thinking that she utterly hated me.

"But . . . But why?" I asked. "AJ, I love you, and you already know that; then why were you afraid to accept your love for me?" I demanded. She seemed so disheartened. It was as if she was internally struggling with something.

"You love me because you don't know my reality. If you knew the truth about me, you would never have fallen in love with me." She was almost sobbing now.

"What reality?! You're wrong, AJ. I love you no matter what your reality is," I said in a firm voice.

"Sid! Just listen to me!" she requested, earnestly.

"No, you listen to me!" I went on to assure her further. "There is nothing that would make me change my mind. Please, AJ. . . Please, accept my love. Give me a chance at least? I will prove to you how much I love you.

"I know you love me, but I don't deserve you."

"What are you saying? It doesn't make any sense. Please AJ, just give me a chance."

After much ado, AJ finally agreed and made me very happy. I promised her that I would never ever hurt her and would always take care of her. I wanted to hold her hand and reassure her of my love, but I hesitated and thought she might find it inappropriate. So, I contented myself by just looking at her. After school, we were standing and chatting in the parking area. Suddenly, my phone rang. My driver was calling me. I answered the call.

"What happened, Sid?" AJ asked.

"Nothing, it's just my driver calling to tell me that he will not be able to pick me up today. My car has broken down," I said while putting my phone in my pocket.

"Oh, so how will you go?"

"I will walk."

"Okay."

"AJ, let me walk you to your house. After that, I will head home."

"Oh, no you don't have to do this. I will go on my own. I don't want my parents to see you with me, actually," AJ said. She looked nervous.

"Okay, at least have a coffee with me before you leave?"

AJ stood there silently. Her behavior was odd. *Her parents must be very strict. That is why she is behaving like this,* I thought to myself.

"AJ, it's just a coffee. You don't have to worry. Your parents will not come to know. Let's go. C'mon!"

After a lot of persuading, she finally agreed to have coffee with me. We walked up to the coffee house in the cool Mussoorie weather. I used to go there on a regular basis with John. The atmosphere inside was warm and cozy. The coffee house was nearly empty. So, we sat at the corner table near a big window that overlooked the beautiful valley. In front of me was lying a menu card.

"AJ, what will you have?" I asked her, scanning the menu.

"Nothing."

"That's not done. You have to take something."

"Actually Sid, I don't like coffee so much."

"Oh, you should have told me. So, let's go somewhere else."

"No, no, let's just talk. But first you should order something for yourself."

"Alright." I stood up and went to place the order. I ordered a cappuccino and brownies, and I went back to AJ.

"AJ, I am so happy that you gave me a chance."

"I am happy, too."

AJ and I were looking into each other eyes. AJ's eyes were dreamy and beautiful. But now and then I could see a shadow of pain in them as well.

"AJ, you are so gorgeous. I feel lucky to have met you." AJ smiled.

"I am lucky too, Sid. You are the most genuine and caring person I have ever met. No one has ever made me feel so loved before." Her eyes were glistening with tears as she said this.

I gathered all my courage to hold her hand and was just about to reach for it when suddenly the waiter came up to our table with our order. I pulled back my extended arm awkwardly and re-adjusted myself in my chair. The waiter placed the order on the table and left.

"AJ, since you don't drink coffee, I ordered some brownies for you."

"Oh, thanks," she said, but barely touched the brownies the whole time we were there.

Some boys entered the coffee house after a while and sat near the center table. When I looked at them, I saw that they were gazing at me with a confused expression on their face.

"AJ, is something wrong with me? Do I look strange?"

"No. Not at all."

"So, why are they staring at me?" I pointed towards the boys.

"I don't know. Let's go from here, Sid. I am not feeling comfortable," AJ said, out of the blue.

"Err. . . But . . . Okay, as you say." I yielded to her request.

We came out from the coffee house instantly. I was still thinking about those boys who were gazing at me. I shook my head to get rid of my thoughts; because of those boys, I did not get to spend much time with AJ. I thought perhaps we should have a do-over. I decided to invite AJ for a dinner date with me tomorrow.

"AJ, will you have dinner with me tomorrow, at my home?" I asked her expectantly.

"At your home?! But. . . What about your parents?" she replied with a strange expression on her face.

"Don't you worry about that. They are going out of town for two days. Now, tell me. Would you have dinner with me tomorrow?"

"Well, in that case, yes!"

"I will pick you up at 8 p.m. from your house," I said.

"No! No! You don't have to! I would come by myself," she replied impatiently, and with a finality that I could not challenge.

"Okay, as you say."

We started walking back. AJ still looked lost. Suddenly, I saw John coming towards our direction. I did not want to him to see me with AJ.

"AJ, my friend John is coming."

"Oh, Sid. I don't want him to know about us."

"I also don't want that. If he comes to know about you and me, he will keep pulling my leg and make my life miserable."

"Oh, don't worry. Why don't you go talk to him, and I will walk to my house?"

"It seems like there is no other way. Okay, then, I will see you tomorrow."

AJ disappeared fast. After talking to John, I also went to my house. As I reached home, I threw my bag on the couch and dozed off on my bed.

The next day, I woke up late as it was a holiday in school. Mom and Dad were out of town for some medical conference. In the afternoon, I sent Rita to her home for one day since I wanted complete privacy. I spent the whole afternoon in making plans for a perfect dinner date with AJ.

I wanted to make pasta for her. She told me once that she liked pasta. But when I entered the kitchen and opened the drawer, I found the packet of pasta completely empty.

I rushed to the supermarket to buy another packet of pasta and some soda cans. I saw John and Nikita shopping together at the store. They were hanging around holding hands. I did not want them to see me, so I hid behind the counter. After five minutes, I saw them leaving, so I swiftly grabbed the one packet of pasta and some soda cans. For dessert, I picked up some chocolate ice cream.

When I was about to leave the supermarket, I saw some fresh, beautiful flowers at the florist's. So, I purchased some of those for AJ as well. I stepped out of the market and saw a cab. I quickly hailed the cab and sat in it. I told the driver the address of my home and drove me there speedily.

Now that the preliminaries were done, I had to address a more difficult problem. I did not really know *how* to make pasta. I only knew how to boil the water. So, I searched for the recipe online on my laptop. Following the recipe very diligently, I finally succeeded in my effort. The pasta was ready!, I went up to my terrace next, to make other preparations. I put candles all around. I decorated the whole terrace with heart-shaped balloons. I was full of excited and nervous energy at the same time.

I went to my room to get ready. After taking a bath, I took out blue jeans and a black shirt from my wardrobe. I changed my clothes and fixed my hair with gel, spending more time on it than usual. I looked in the mirror. I thought I looked decent enough. I sprayed my favourite rose perfume on my clothes. Before leaving the room, I once again looked in the mirror to make sure everything was in place. Then, I went to the kitchen. I took out the pasta from the oven and garnished it with cheese. I had also prepared a salad. I arranged all the food on a tray and kept it on standby. I took out our fancy bone china plates and crystal glasses from my mother's expensive crockery set.

I was waiting for AJ anxiously. Suddenly, the bell rang. I ran happily towards the door. As I opened the door, I saw a young boy with dark black hair standing there.

"Sir, have you ordered a pizza?" he asked wearily.

"No," I replied.

"Oh, sorry. Sir, can you tell me where this address is?" He showed me a pink slip.

"It's the next house."

"Thank you, sir, and sorry for disturbing you."

"It's okay. No problem."

I came back inside and sat on my sofa. The bell rang again. I opened the door, and there she was finally, standing at my doorstep. She was wearing a short red dress with black heels. She looked stunning. I tried to keep my mouth from dropping open.

Chapter 5

Dinner Date

"AJ, you look gorgeous," I complimented her.

"Thank you," she said beaming. "You too are looking handsome."

"Thanks. Please come in." I took her to my drawing-room.

AJ sat on the sofa. I served her the soda and sat next to her. I kept looking at her. She smiled nervously, and after a short silence, I said, "AJ, let's go to my terrace. I have a surprise for you."

"Surprise?" she said in a polite tone. Her smile grew wider.

"Yes," I replied, excitedly.

We both walked towards the stairs. I grabbed my black jacket. Suddenly, my phone rang loudly, but I did not pay attention.

"Your phone is ringing," AJ said.

"I know." I took out the phone from my pocket.

"Answer it, then," AJ nodded towards my phone.

"No! I won't pick it up. I don't want anybody to disturb us. I just want to spend this time with you alone without any disturbance," I said while switching off the phone.

"You are so sweet," AJ praised.

"Thanks, let's go then."

My excitement was rising with every minute passing.

"AJ, please close your eyes," I requested.

"Why?" she asked, her eyes getting wider.

"Please."

"Okay."

I opened the gate of the terrace, excitedly.

"AJ, open your eyes."

AJ's eyes sparkled with happiness. I had decorated the roof in Valentine's Day theme even though it was not Valentine's Day. AJ and I stepped inside the gate. I turned on the slow romantic music on my Bluetooth speakers.

"Oh! Sid, it's all so beautiful—the music and the decoration."

"When you hang around angels such as yourself, you're influenced to do good things."

AJ smiled sweetly. We both sat in our chairs. I gave her the flowers which I bought for her from the market.

"Thanks, Sid. These are my favourite flowers." I had given her white roses.

"AJ, I have to go downstairs."

"Why?" she asked politely.

"I am going downstairs to bring the food."

"Oh, okay."

I came back with the food tray. I placed the plates on the table, and I served AJ the pasta and salad. I also poured soda into the glasses. We both started talking and eating peacefully. The weather was very pleasant with a cool breeze blowing constantly. The sky above was clear. One could easily see the bright shining stars and the moon which was bright as a smile. It was perfect for a dinner date out on the terrace.

"The pasta is very nice. I really liked it." She liked the pasta, but for some strange reason, I was suspicious because since I was busy setting everything up and making frequent trips to the kitchen to get the seasonings and other things, I did not actually see her eating.

"Have some more if you like it so much." I served her some more pasta, leaving my silly suspicion behind since her plate was clearly empty.

"Who has made this?" AJ asked while looking at me.

"I have made this myself."

"Really? Do you know how to cook?" she questioned, surprised.

"No. I read the recipe online."

"I am impressed," she said.

AJ and I were looking into each other eyes adoringly. Her generous and warm eyes were killing me. Suddenly, I noticed that her eyes were becoming wet.

"Are you crying, AJ?" I asked. I was very concerned.

"No, I am not crying. These are just happy tears."

I was about to hold her hand. But suddenly, I heard somebody calling my name.

"Sid! Sid! Sid! Are you there?"

When I looked towards the voice, I saw my mom standing right there in front of me on the terrace. She seemed annoyed. She was staring at me, angrily.

"Mom!!! What are you doing here? You were supposed to be at the medical conference in Dehradun!" I asked.

"We changed our program. Do you have any problem? Where is your phone? I was calling you," she yelled.

"Sorry, Mom. I couldn't take your call then. But please, can we speak later? I'm trying to have a romantic dinner here, so if you don't mind . . ."

"Oh! You're having a romantic dinner all alone?" My mom asked with a raised eyebrow.

"Alone? What are you talking about? Can't you see? AJ is sitting right here with me," I replied in exasperation, still looking at my mother.

"No, I can't see your imaginary girlfriend," she said, tauntingly.

"Mom, she is sitting right next to me." I turned my face to look at AJ, but she was not there!

"When you're done having dinner with your imaginary girlfriend, join your Dad and me for a movie in our room, if you're up for it," she offered.

"Mom, wait," I insisted.

"Bye, Sid," she replied tersely and left.

Where is she! Where did she go? Did something happen to her? She must have become nervous due to my mom yelling. But how could she disappear like that? I was confounded.

"Sid?"

"Oh! AJ, you are still here! I thought you took off," I breathed a sigh of relief.

"Do you really think I would take off without saying goodbye to you?" No, I just went to the toilet," she replied.

"But when my mom didn't see you here, she thought I had gone mad. She thought I was having this romantic dinner all alone with myself. Wait, I will call her up right now, then she will believe me," I explained.

"Don't ruin the moment, Sid. I just want to be alone with you. Is that all right?" she asked all starry-eyed.

"But what about my mom's misunderstanding?"

"You can resolve it later, can't you?" she requested.

"Yes, I can. Sure. Let me take a selfie with you so that I can show it to Mom later. "Smile, please," I clicked a picture quickly.

"Let me see this picture first," she demanded.

"Okay, here, take a look." She seemed tensed when she saw the picture.

"Now give me the phone."

"No," she refused.

"Give it to me," I snatched my phone from her hands in jest. "I too want to see the picture."

I ran away from her with my phone, laughing. The moment I turned around, I realized, AJ was nowhere to be seen!

"AJ! AJ! AJ! Where are you?" Suddenly, my heart sank. I searched for her all over the terrace, but I could not find her anywhere. My blood froze. I did not understand what was happening. She was right there in front of me! How could she just disappear into thin air like that! It was impossible! Was she all right?

I went downstairs and asked my mom about AJ. Mom was watching a funny movie with my dad, and her anger seemed to have subsided. Mom came towards me. She laughed and replied. "Are you still playing that 'invisible girlfriend' game of yours?

"No, Mom! This time I have proof! Here, see this picture." I showed her the selfie.

"Oh! Yes, you are right there. It is a very nice picture of you . . . and your invisible girlfriend!" She laughed again.

"What are you saying, Mom? Show me the picture." I took the phone from her hand and looked at the picture. I was shocked! It was just a picture of me and an empty chair. A chill went down to my spine.

"If you are done, let us go. Your father is waiting," Mom nudged me to come with her.

I mindlessly followed my Mom and sat on the corner sofa in my parent's room. But I was in utter shock. I did not know what to do. I was feeling very disoriented, confused and scared. I could not even explain my dilemma to anyone. I felt helpless.

Chapter 6

The Truth

I lay on my bed, thinking about the incident with AJ on the terrace a few hours ago. I glanced at the clock on my dashboard. It was 3 o' clock. The rest of the night passed in heavy mental and emotional strain. It was impossible for me to believe what I saw in that picture.

I woke up late in the morning the next day. I had a throbbing headache due to the lack of sleep. My eyes felt sore and painful. Somehow, I got ready and went downstairs. I was getting late for school.

"Sid, you are late for school," Mom informed.

"I know, Mom," I said in a weak voice.

"Son, eat something before leaving," Dad said.

"I am not hungry, Dad. I will eat something at school."

My mom packed some sandwiches for me. My driver dropped me at the school. I made my way to the History class in a daze. I did not even realize that the lecture had already started when I first walked into the classroom.

"Thank you for joining us, Mr. Sid," Mr. Roy said in a disparaging tone.

I was jolted out of my slumber and hurried to my seat. I realized AJ was not there; I felt a twinge of horror. I was becoming restless with every passing moment. Mr. Roy was staring at me constantly, but I did not pay attention. I went to the cafeteria in hopes of finding AJ. But I came back disappointed. The rest of my day in school passed in a blur. When I went home, Mom was sitting in the garden, working on her laptop.

"How was your day, dear?" Mom asked.

"Fine," I lied. My voice was weak.

She did not look convinced. I put my bag on the table and sat down on the chair. I felt miserable. Rita brought a cup of tea for Mom and a glass of orange juice for me.

"Mom, I have a headache. Please give me a painkiller."

"Had you eaten those sandwiches that I gave you in the morning?"

"No, Mom. I didn't eat anything. I was not feeling well."

"Sid, you have to eat something before the medicine."

"Rita, bring something for Sid," Mom said to Rita.

After I had something, Mom gave me a painkiller. She instructed me to take rest in my room, so I headed there. After changing my clothes, I lay down on my bed. I was in such a miserable state. I had never felt that helpless in my whole life. I did not know anything about my beloved AJ. My predicament was so inexplicable. I could not make anyone understand what I was going through. *Who would believe me?* I myself doubted my own sanity. How could someone disappear like this! Where are you, AJ?

Two days had passed, and I did not hear from her. It was getting unbearable, and I could not sit idle any longer. I had to do something. I had to find out what had happened!

I thought of going to my school administration office and asking them for AJ's house address. When I went to the office, I found that it had closed earlier than usual that day. When I was going back to my class, dejected I spotted Nikita on the way. She was sitting alone in the cafeteria, making some notes. Her books were spread all over the table. I thought of asking her about AJ.

"Hey, Nikita," I said.

"Hey, Sid," she replied while sipping her coffee.

"Nikita, have you seen AJ?" I asked.

"AJ, who?" she replied with a weird expression.

"My girlfriend," I said while sitting on a chair next to her.

"Your girlfriend? I didn't know you had a girlfriend," she replied. She looked surprised.

"I do have a girlfriend, and her name is AJ. Do you know where she is?"

Suddenly, her phone rang loudly. She took out her phone from her pink designer bag.

"Nikita, please. Could you tell me first?" I requested.

"Sid, my mom is calling. I have to take this call."

She started talking to her Mom on the phone. Meanwhile, I was wondering how she could forget AJ? All three of us went to same class every day. I was getting restless. She hung up the phone and turned to me.

"Nikita, how can you forget about AJ?!" I asked. I was frustrated.

"Oh! AJ. . . Right! Now I remember! Yes, she was in our class. But. . . how can she be your girlfriend, Sid? She is dead," she said while casually putting her phone back in her bag.

"Dead?!" I was dumbfounded.

"Yes, she died. Don't you know?" she replied, confidently.

"What are you saying, Nikita? How can she be dead?" I demanded.

"What do you mean?" She looked surprised.

I shook my head in confusion. "I mean . . . how . . . how and when she did this happen?" I was trying hard to make sense of what she was saying and somehow trying to control my restless and overwhelming feelings.

"On her first day of school itself," she responded. "Do you remember she left earlier that day?"

"Yes," I replied, recalling that day.

"Actually, her parents had come to pick her up, and when they were going back to their home, suddenly a big truck came out of nowhere and crashed into their car. The whole family died on the spot," she explained. Her tone was very matter-of-fact, and it sent chills down my spine.

"Nikita, what. . . what are you saying? This can't be t. . . true. . . " I stammered. I was in shock. "You are joking, right? Tell me that you are joking."

"No. Are you mad? Why would I joke about this? Everybody in the school knows about this incident," she said, frowning.

"Oh! My God" I said, under my breath.

I felt like I was going to faint. I thought to myself: *How had I not heard about this? Who was it that I was dating all this while? Is that why everyone was laughing at me that day when I confessed my feelings for her? Because they just saw me, alone, talking to an empty chair? Mom was also right that day she saw me alone on the terrace. Everybody must have thought that I am mad. Was I really hanging around with the ghost of AJ? I realized I never saw AJ with anyone. She was always alone. When we went to the coffee shop, she never had anything to eat. On the terrace also, I never really saw her eating that pasta! I had never even touched her hand ever.* Everything was coming back to me now.

I decided to find AJ, at any cost. Whoever she was, whatever she was, she owed me an answer!

I was shivering and feeling very scared. But at the same time, I was also strangely feeling abandoned, deserted and betrayed by someone I had loved dearly. I wanted to find her, but I did not know where to start. Suddenly, it started raining heavily. After the school, I went back to my house, still in denial, and still trying to process what I had just found out.

Chapter 7

Reliving the Past

𝒥t was 2 o' clock in the night, and I was sitting on the couch, looking out of the window. I was trying very hard to believe that the person I was dating all this while and had fallen so deeply in love with, was actually dead, that I had been going around with a ghost! How could someone ever reconcile with something like that? My head was throbbing with pain. So, I went to the kitchen and took out a bottle of water from the fridge. After drinking some water, I went back to my room and sat down on my couch again.

It was dark, cold and foggy outside. Suddenly, I saw a shadow outside my window. I felt as if that shadow was trying to pull me out of the sofa. Willingly or unwillingly, I found myself getting up from the sofa, going downstairs and then walking outside from the front door of the house. I was scared, but I continued to follow the shadow. It was dark outside, but the moonlight was casting a mysterious gleam over the night. Dogs were barking in the distance. I was fearful of where this shadow may lead me, but I do not know why I kept following it. Something about it seemed familiar. I felt like the shadow was in deep sorrow and pain and wanted to tell me something. I felt connected to it.

After walking for some time, I reached a secluded and silent place, away from the city. The place was as silent as death. I had never seen that place before in my whole life. My heartbeat rose incredibly. I had sweat on my palms. I noticed that the shadow in front of me had suddenly disappeared, and I stopped right there. Then, I heard a voice. *Sid . . . Sid . . . Sid . . .* It was AJ's voice! But when I turned towards the voice, I saw nobody.

"Where are you, AJ?" I demanded.

"I am standing in front of you," she replied. Her voice was weak.

"But I can't see you!" I said.

"Yes, you will not be able to see me anymore. I am dead, Sid," she replied in a low morose tone.

I knew she was dead, but when I heard it from her, I felt a sharp pain in my heart. I shook my head, and I asked, "I know that now, AJ. But why can't I see you now when I could before?"

"It's because of the treaty," she replied.

"Which treaty? What are you talking about? Tell me everything! I need some answers!" I demanded, frustrated.

"For that, I have to tell you my story from the beginning," she said.

"Yes. Please. Go ahead; I am listening," I replied, dreading what she would say.

"This is all happening because of my parents."

"Your parents?"

"Yes."

Thus, she began her story. She told me that her parents never loved her. That she had a difficult childhood. Her parents used to mentally and physically torture her. They had beaten her many times. All because she was a girl. When her mother was pregnant, everyone told her it was a boy. They always wanted a boy and were overjoyed at the thought. But when she was born, their hopes of having a boy were shattered. They hated her intensely. They always treated her as a liability. They never took her out of the house or to the frequent parties they went to and even when someone came to their home, they always introduce her as their maid.

Her voice was shaking while talking. She told me that she used to believe that once her parents had a boy, they will stop torturing her, but that did not happen even after the birth of her brother. They hated her even more. So much so that they wished for AJ's death.

She told me that one day her parents sent their brother out of the house on a false pretext. Since she was alone at home, they tried to kill her by making her eat poisoned curd.

"Oh my God!"

"I ate that poisoned curd. After eating the curd, my throat started closing up. I started to feel suffocated. My head was rolling, and I fell on the floor. I was begging for help. But my parents just stood there in the corner quietly waiting for me to die. They had a smile on their cruel face."

"Oh my God, AJ! Then, what happened? Who saved you?"

"Luckily, my grandmother came to our house. She had a key to the house, so she came directly inside. She saw me lying on the floor, frothing at the mouth, begging for help. She called the ambulance and took me to the hospital swiftly. My parents pretended they did not know what was happening," she explained.

"Oh! So where is your grandmother now?"

"She died three years ago from an asthma attack. But I am suspicious about the circumstances of her death."

"Suspicious of what?"

"Of my parents' involvement in her death. I think they murdered her."

"What! Why do you think that?"

"Because one day before her death, she changed her will and made me the sole owner of the whole property that belongs to our family. She gave nothing to my parents." After a pause, she continued, "Moreover, she also stated in the will that if I die, the property will go to charity. She didn't want my parents to try and kill me again."

"Then what happened?"

"I was only fifteen when she died. My parents pulled some tricks with the help of our family lawyer, and they became the caretaker of the property until I turned eighteen."

"Oh! How clever and cruel they are." I felt an intense hatred towards AJ's parents.

She told me that her grandmother really loved her, but after she died, AJ felt utterly alone. Her parents did not even let her meet her brother. She was totally alone. In such circumstances, she desperately craved for true love, and when she saw me for the first time, she fell in love with me. She thought that I would be the one who could give her the love she deserved, but fate had something else planned for her. She died before she could realize her dream of being truly loved by someone.

"AJ . . . I can't express how I am feeling right now. How can fate be so cruel? But, I don't understand. How can you be here if you are dead? How could I see you when the rest of the people can't?" I asked.

Suddenly, AJ yelled, "Go from here Sid! Go! Run!" She sounded petrified.

"What's going on AJ?" I asked, panicking. The night sky suddenly darkened further; it was frightening.

"I will tell you tomorrow," she replied in a whisper.

"But . . . But. . . " I objected.

"Meet me tomorrow, behind our school at 1.30 a.m., I will explain everything to you," she promised.

"AJ, listen to me, please," I said.

"Just go from here quickly, please," she insisted. "It's not safe to talk here right now. I will meet you tomorrow, I promise."

I did not want to go, but I left the place in a hurry as AJ directed, with a hope of seeing her again. I went back to my house and lay down on my bed.

Chapter 8

Answers

*W*hen I opened my eyes the next morning, I felt that everything in my life had transformed in the duration of a single night. I jumped out of my bed and looked out of the window. The weather outside was cold and foggy. I went to the bathroom, and after brushing my teeth, I took a long warm bath. I changed my clothes and got ready.

I unplugged my phone from charging point and put it in the right pocket of my jeans. I closed the door of my room and went downstairs. I saw my parents going through their usual morning routine. My mom was putting some documents in her handbag, and my dad was sitting at the dining table eating his breakfast.

"Good morning, Mom and Dad," I said.

"Good morning, son," Mom and Dad replied in unison.

"I thought you were sleeping," Mom said.

"No, I woke up early."

"Oh, thats good. We have to go to the hospital early today."

"Why are you going early today?"

"There is an emergency case at the hospital."

"Oh."

"Sid, we will have to stay at the hospital today and will be back by tomorrow morning. Rita too is on holiday today. She has gone to her sister's house. Will you be able to manage?"

"I will manage, Mom," I assured.

"I have made some sandwiches for you, do eat them," Mom warned.

"Okay, Mom," I replied.

"Sid, it's really cold. Wear some warm clothes if you don't want to fall ill," Dad advised.

"I will, Dad."

"Hurry up, honey. We are getting late," Dad said to Mom while looking at his wristwatch.

"One minute, please," she said, picking up her purse.

Mom and Dad hugged me and left for the hospital. I went up to my room and took out my favorite blue jacket from my wardrobe and wore it while coming down the stairs. I went and sat on the sofa of my drawing-room feeling alone and frazzled. I was thinking about AJ and spent the rest of my day worrying constantly.

I took out the sandwich Mom had put in the fridge and put them in the grill machine. I poured a glass of orange juice as well. After eating, I went to my room, slumped on my couch and kept looking anxiously at the clock. It was getting harder and harder for me to pass the time. I wanted to meet AJ.

Beeb . . . Beeb . . .

"Oh my God, it's 1.45 a.m.! I am already fifteen minutes late; how could I doze off in this situation?" I left my home in a hurry. It was dark and cloudy, and the roads were slippery because of the rain. I turned on the flashlight of my phone and started walking as fast as I could. When I reached there, I started searching for AJ.

"AJ! AJ! Where are you?" I called out her name loudly.

"I am here, in front of you," she replied in a low voice.

"I still can't see you," I said. I was feeling torn up inside. I turned off the flashlight of my phone.

"Anyway, now please tell me about that treaty you were talking about yesterday," I asked.

"Yes, the treaty . . ." she replied in a weak tone. "The accident in which I died was brutal. My soul left my mortal body instantly with the deadly impact of the accident. Somehow, after a while, I found myself looking at my own dead body immersed in blood, lying lifeless on the road. Next to me lay my parents and my younger brother in a similar condition. I was so disoriented and frightened. I didn't understand anything. It took me a long time to understand and accept that I was actually dead. Suddenly, I saw blue flashes of light that almost blinded me. It was appearing right in front of me, slowly getting brighter. I felt that the light was dragging me towards it. I was petrified and helpless." She paused for a second.

"Then, what happened?" I asked, desperately.

"I was screaming, and pleading: *Don't take me, don't take me please, I beg of you. I have never experienced true love in my whole life; please let me experience it once . . . my parents always tortured me . . . please don't take me without me feeling loved at least once in my life*, I was begging."

The sky was overcast and it started raining again. I felt so emotional because of all the pain she had to go through her life and even after it. How much she had suffered at such a young age! I shook my head in disbelief.

"Suddenly, I heard a voice," she said.

"What voice?" I asked. A curious sensation overwhelmed me.

"It was coming from the Blue Light. However, I couldn't tell whether the voice was male or female. But it was gentle and understanding. It said, *Don't cry AJ. But your time on earth is over.* I was in denial. I kept saying no. I begged the Light: *Please let me experience true love once, please. I will not ask for anything else. I just want to know how being loved feels. Please.* Suddenly, it stopped dragging me," she explained.

"I did not hear anything till some time. Then, the voice from the light said: *Okay, AJ. Because you are a pure soul, I will give you a chance. But you have to make a treaty with me.* When I asked about the nature of the treaty, it said: *Only your true love will be able to see you, but if he comes to know about your reality, you will become invisible to him as well. After that, you will have to come with me when I come back for you,* It warned me sternly.

"I asked, *Okay, but what if he never comes to know about my reality?*

Even then, I will come back to take you after some time, It told me in a firm tone."

"Oh! Is that why I can't see you anymore?" I asked.

"Yes."

"Oh, you have been through a lot, AJ." I could hear her crying. I wanted to hug her.

"One more thing. Why did you tell me to leave in a hurry yesterday?"

"Because of my parents," she replied.

"Your parents? But they are dead, right?" I asked.

"Yes, they died, but they also became like me, and now they are hounding me even after death." She replied in a scared tone.

My jaw dropped when I heard that.

"Oh my God, what are you saying? Your parents became ghosts as well?!" I was dumbfounded.

"Yes," she replied.

"What will you do now?" I asked, concerned.

"Nothing, I will just wait for that Blue Light to come back and take me," she said in a low voice.

"What about your parents, then? What if they keep hounding you till then?" I asked.

"Once I go away from here, they will never be able to bother me," she replied.

I stood there in silence, stunned.

Chapter 9

Good Bye

"*L*et me help you until then; I know I can't see you, but I can hear you, so I am sure I can be of some help," I insisted.

"No," she replied with hesitation.

"Why?" I demanded.

"Sid, we have to separate one day, and it will be easier if we do it right now," she said. I could hear her sniffling. She was crying.

"No, AJ. Please, I can't live without you," I replied, crestfallen.

"No, Sid! Please understand. I cannot ruin your life anymore. Since the moment I asked for another chance at experiencing love, I have felt nothing but regret. I became selfish at that moment, but not anymore. I cannot ruin your life," AJ continued. "I should have known that I will not be able to reciprocate your love in a manner you deserved. But I got swayed by my emotions. I still I came to you, and I am sorry for that."

"Don't be sorry AJ, because I am not. You are the best thing that ever happened to me, and I love you very much," I reassured her.

"Yes, I know that Sid, but now the ghosts of my parents are also out there; they can hurt you if they saw you with me, so please, you must let me go," she pleaded. Her voice was weak.

"No, please don't leave me; I don't know how much time you have, but at least you can spend the rest of your time on earth with me," I pleaded. I had tears in my eyes.

"No, it will hurt you more. Goodbye Sid, and I'm sorry once again."

"No!" AJ! AJ! AJ! Please at least spend some time with me. I think I deserve some of your time before you leave me forever," I begged.

"If things were in my hands, I would have given you all the time in the world," AJ replied, emotionally overwhelmed.

Finally, after my incessant pleading, AJ agreed to spend some time with me. The wind was blowing softly. I sat down on a bench.

"AJ, come sit with me."

"I am already sitting next to you."

"I wish I could see you," I said with a heavy heart.

Suddenly, I heard some voices coming from behind the tree. I was frightened. But when I looked in that direction, nobody was there.

"AJ, did you hear a voice?" I asked.

"No. I did not."

"Oh, okay."

"Did you hear anything? She sounded suspicious.

"Yes."

"From where?

"From behind the tree." I nodded towards the tree. "Why? Who do you think it is?" I asked.

"I think my parents are here," she replied.

"What!" I gulped.

"Are you sure?"

"No. But let me check once. You keep sitting here. I am going to check," AJ instructed.

"I am coming with you. If your parents are here, then they can harm both of us in some way."

"Alright." she agreed. We walked together, looking around carefully.

"AJ. Did you see them?"

"No, I didn't. They are not here. I checked the whole place."

"Oh, thank God." I sighed. AJ and I sat down on the bench again. We started talking.

"AJ, I never believed in love at first sight. But when I saw you that day on the street, I fell for you instantly."

"But I thought you saw me in the class for the first time," she said, surprised.

"No, that was the second time."

"I always believed in love at first sight. I also fell for you when I saw you for the first time," AJ told me.

I was so happy when I heard that. "You saw me for the first time in the History class, right?"

"No," she said, politely.

"What? Then when did you see me?" I was bewildered.

"Three months ago, my parents were searching for a home in your town. They brought me here with them. I was sitting at a home broker's office, and I saw you crossing the street."

"Oh!"

"Just with the one glimpse of you, I felt a strange but strong connection with you. I stood up and went outside, but you were gone by then. I looked all around, but I didn't find you."

"I wish we could have met that day itself. Who knows, things would have been different then." I said meekly.

"Yes, I wish that too."

"AJ, I want to ask something."

"Yes?" "One day I saw you outside my house, and when I asked you about the same, you told me that you went for a picnic with your parents."

"Yes. Actually Sid, that day I had come to see you. I wanted to tell you everything. Because only you were able to see me and since the Blue Light had told me that only my true love would able to see me, I knew you were the one. Also, what I felt for you could not be anything else but true love."

"Hmm . . ."

"I knew you loved me truly. So, I wanted to tell you the whole truth. But at the last minute, I didn't have the courage to talk to you. So, I went away."

"Oh." I sat there wishing I could hold her hand just once.

"Sid, I have to go know."

"Please AJ, stay with me till that light comes to take you," I requested again.

"I wish I could stay," AJ said, under her breath.

"Then stay."

"Sid, I must go. Don't make it harder for me and you as well. All I ever wanted is to be loved by someone like you. I am glad I experienced that feeling at least for some time. But that is all that my destiny will allow me. Goodbye Sid. I will always wish for your best.

"AJ! AJ!" I was calling her name, but she did not reply. I assumed that she had gone.

Tears were rolling down my face now. I sat on the bench for some time. I was crying miserably. I felt like somebody had stabbed my heart. I was in pain and breathing heavily.

I was about to leave, when suddenly I heard some voices again. I looked up to see from where the voices were coming, but I could not see anything because of the darkness that had engulfed me. The street lights were not working as well. So, I turned on the flashlight of my phone to look clearly, but I did not see anyone. I looked at my wristwatch; it was 3.30 a.m. I heard some more voices, but this time more clearly.

"AJ, is that you?"

Nobody replied. I was scared; my heart beat started to increase.

I got up and started walking. As I walked, I felt that someone was following me. I was scared and was sweat profusely. Then, I heard a male voice.

"Sid! Sid!"

I did not look back and started running instantly. I just wanted to reach my home. I was running so fast that I was able to hear my heart beat clearly against my chest. It started raining again, and the roads become more slippery.

By a wicked twist of fate, I slipped on a rock and fell backwards, and hit my back on another rock. I lay there in severe pain. As I tried to get up, I heard that male voice again.

"Sid! Sid!"

When I looked up, nobody was there.

"Sid!"

"Who are you? Why are you following me?" I asked in a scared voice.

"We are AJ's parents," they replied together.

Chapter 10
An Accident

"*A*J's parents!" I exclaimed. I was dumbfounded.

My heart skipped a beat. I was scared as hell. I stood up and started running as fast as I could. They kept calling my name, but I did not look back.

I was running like the wind. I was so scared that I did not notice that a big white car was coming towards me at full speed, and before I knew it, I got hit by that car. I screamed as it knocked me hard and thrust me to the pavement on the side. I became unconscious as I fell.

"Sid! Sid."

My mom was calling my name repeatedly, her voice was weak and desperate. "Mom," I said in a weak tone. I opened my eyes in an unfamiliar place. I had pain all over my body. I saw my dad was standing in a corner, talking to someone.

"Oh, Sid, thank God you regained consciousness," she replied. She seemed happy.

"What? Where am I?" I asked in a weak voice.

"In the hospital son, you met with an accident this morning," Dad replied while coming towards me. He looked concerned.

I began slowly to come to my senses. All at once, I remembered everything that happened to me in the morning. I remembered about AJ's parents. I shook my head. My mouth and throat were dry. Next to my bed, stood a three-drawer nightstand, and on the top was a glass filled with water and a remote control for the television.

"Mom, please give me a glass of water."

My mom picked up the glass of water from the nightstand and helped me drink it. I was admitted to my parent's hospital, I realized. The private room I occupied was the most expensive room in the hospital. A big television hung on the wall. The air was scented with perfume, and the seats for the family members were wide and comfortable. Every surface was dustless.

The walls had white wallpaper with a flower design on it. There were vases of flower and beautiful framed pieces of art on the wall.

"Sid, how are you feeling now?" Mom asked, worried.

"Better, Mom. But, I have pain all over my body," I replied in a low voice.

"Don't worry, I will give you painkillers for that," she said.

"Okay, Mom, one more thing, when will I get discharged?" I inquired.

"Tomorrow morning, son," she promised.

"Oh, no! Mom can't you discharge me today?" I requested.

"No, son. you are still weak, I can't discharge you, please understand," she replied.

"Okay Mom, as you say."

"Take rest son, your dad and I are going out of the room to check on other patients."

Mom gave me a kiss on the forehead before leaving.

A nurse came to my room after they left. She checked my blood pressure and gave me an injection. After the nurse went outside, I was all alone in the room. I was thinking about the incident.

"Hey, Sid." I heard a familiar voice

"Hey, John! What are you doing here?"

"I heard about your accident. So, I came to meet you." he continued. "How are you feeling?" He seemed genuinely worried.

"I am fine now," I replied weakly.

"That's good. Sid, I want to ask you something."

"What do you want to ask?"

"Nikita told me that you were asking her about the girl who died, AJ. You told her that she is your girlfriend? And now, this accident. What's going on with you my friend."

I was stunned. I didn't know what to reply. Suddenly, my mom entered the room. And I breathed a sigh of relief.

"Hello, aunty," John greeted my mom.

"Hello, John. How are you?"

"I am good."

"John, I'm sorry but I have to give him an injection. So, you have to go outside.

"Oh, no problem, aunty. I am just leaving."

"I will talk to you at school," John said to me.

John left the room. I thanked God for saving me. Mom gave me an injection. Due to the heavy dose of painkillers and the injuries, I was feeling sleepy and groggy. I didn't know when I fell asleep.

I opened my eyes to a familiar place. I was aware that I was dreaming. I saw AJ sitting on a bench. She was wearing a long white gown. She looked gorgeous and angelic as always. She seemed happy and peaceful. She called me by my name: "Sid! Sid!"

"Come and sit with me," she requested, politely.

"Hey, AJ," I replied, merrily. I was wearing white jeans with a pink shirt. My hair was fixed perfectly. I was looking tidy.

I sat next to her. She held my hand tightly and looked into my eyes romantically. The weather was pleasant and the wind was blowing softly. The fragrance of the flowers was spread in the air all around the place. We were talking to each other. Both of us were very happy together. We didn't want to be separated. I was just about to hug her when suddenly, my phone rang waking me up. I looked up at the clock, it was 7.30 p.m. I did not want to wake up from my dream. It was so beautiful and felt so real.

I looked out of my room's window, it was getting darker. I was trying to sleep again in hopes of meeting AJ in my dream, but I couldn't fall asleep after that. I was restless. Suddenly, I heard some voices again.

"Hey, Sid," A voice came. I instantly recognized that voice, it was AJ's father.

"What do you want from me? Why are you hounding me?" I asked, frustrated and overwhelmed with fright.

"We want to . . . "

I interrupted, "We? Who . . . who else is with you?" I was sweating profusely. My voice was shaking but still I tried hard to be bold and brave and hold my ground. "My wife," he replied.

"Why are you doing this now, your daughter who you people never loved, is already dead? You tortured her when she was alive, at least leave her alone now. She told me everything about you."

"But listen to us once, please," they said.

"Why should I listen? You people tortured my AJ. Just go from here. Leave me alone."

"Yes, you are right, but we realized our mistakes, and now we want to apologize to her," they said sounding mournful.

"Apologize??" I was shocked.

Chapter 11

An Apology

"Oh! You want to apologize now?" I asked, sarcastically. I was suspicious of their motives.

"Yes, we really want to apologize to her; help us, please," they pleaded.

"I am not going to help you. I can't trust you, and I don't understand why you changed your heart, all of a sudden," I demanded in a strong voice.

"Sid, when we died, we saw our life in a series of flashes and it was horrible. And we realized how badly we treated our daughter. We were wrong," they replied. I could hear them weeping.

"No! No! I can't trust you," I yelled.

"Please! Sid, help us please, this is our last chance to apologize," they insisted.

"No! No! Go from here right now."

They were pleading and crying badly. My heart melted, and I thought AJ would be happy to know that her parents realized their mistakes, and she will go from earth peaceful.

I said, "Wait. . . Okay . . . I will help you."

"Oh! Thanks, Sid."

"But how can I help you?"

"For that, you have to come with us."

"Where?" I asked with an astonished expression on my face.

"Actually, Sid, whenever we have tried to talk to AJ, she has ran away. If she saw you with us, I think she will talk to us," they explained.

"You, people are right. Let's go then, but wait, my parents are just outside. What if they saw me?" I questioned.

"Where are they?"

"They are outside the room."

I slightly opened the door of my room and peeped outside. I saw my parents were sleeping in the waiting area. The corridor was empty.

"They are sleeping," I told AJ's parents.

"Oh! That's good. Now you can come with us safely."

"Yes," I agreed.

I changed my hospital clothes and took out my phone from the drawer. I had pain all over my body. I took two painkillers with a glass of water. I somehow managed to go out from the hospital without being noticed. The guard at the gate was sleeping. I was very happy, I thought that now finally AJ would get what she deserved from her parents. We headed towards the area behind my school because that was the place where I met AJ the last time. The school was just five minutes away from the hospital. I was walking slowly.

When we were on the way I thought what if that Blue Light had already taken her away, and then all this will go in vain. She would never be get to know that her parents wanted to apologize to her. The thought of not listening to her voice again killed me inside. I was praying to God fervently.

"We have reached," they said.

We started searching for AJ. Actually, only they could do that because only they could see her, and I couldn't, but I was calling her name repeatedly, "AJ! AJ! Where are you?"

"I think she is not here," AJ's father said.

"Let me try once again," I requested.

"AJ! AJ!" I called her again.

"She is not here."

"Where is she, then?"

"We know where she could be," they said.

They took me to a strange place. That place was about two kilometers away from the jungle. When we reached the place, it was dark and gloomy. It was so quiet that I could easily hear the sound of the wind whispering through the trees. The dogs were barking, and the owls were screaming. The atmosphere of that place was freaky. It was near the old lake where no one ever went.

"AJ! AJ!"

Suddenly, I heard her beautiful voice, and I thanked God that she was still here.

"Sid! What are you doing with them!?" she exclaimed. She was sounding upset and scared.

"AJ, don't worry. They want to apologize to you," I explained to her.

"Apologize? What rubbish! They have fooled you, Sid. They would never apologize to me. Their hatred knows no boundary. They hate me in the after-life as well," she said convinced of her parent's evil nature.

"But! But! They told me that they wanted to apologize."

Suddenly, AJ's parent's burst into laughter. They were laughing loudly and called me stupid. I was dumbfounded.

"Oh! Our poor daughter, she knows us so well, yes, we don't want to apologize to this foul girl who ruined our lives. We are here to steal her happiness instead! Her happiness lies in you! We are going to kill Siddharth! We will never let you live peacefully," they said, while laughing loudly.

"Why are you doing this? Why do you want to kill me?" I demanded.

"You don't get it, Sid! You are a stupid boy. We can't see her happy and now you are the reason for her happiness, so we will snatch it from her," they replied in a tone that reverberated across the forest.

"Then why didn't you kill me at the hospital? I was alone, you could have easily killed me there," I asked, trying to gain some courage.

"Because we wanted to kill you in front of AJ."

"Kill me then," I urged them. "I am not afraid of you, anymore."

"Sid, what are you saying?" AJ interrupted.

"Let them kill me, we both will go from here, and live peacefully up there," I requested AJ.

"No! I want you to live a happy life."

"No! AJ, I anyway can't live without you."

"Sid, please don't do this; you are hurting me," she pleaded. "Think about your parents. What will they do without you?"

"Shut up you two! We are going to kill him whether he wants it or not," they said in a vengeful voice.

"Run! Sid, run!" AJ shouted.

"Not without you! Come with me!" I screamed.

I started running as fast as I could, and I knew AJ was following me. We were scared and helpless. We didn't know what to do.

"We will not leave you now. Run as fast as you can. We will find you and kill you." They were sniggering.

"Sid! Run fast. They are following us," AJ shouted.

Chapter 12

The Jungle

$\mathcal{W}$e were running as fast as we could. The beating of my heart was the only sound I could hear. We were running so fast that we did not know where we were going or how to go there; we did not know how we got out from there, we only knew that we were running as fast as we could.

After a while, when I stopped to look around, it was so dark that I was not able to see anything, but I could smell wet wood and the grass beneath my feet too was wet and cold. I assumed that we had entered a jungle again.

I never liked the jungle. There was something creepy about it. When I was only ten years old, I went to a jungle safari with my parents and I got lost in the jungle. Since that day, I had again ventured near a jungle. I was terrified, but I wouldn't let it show on my face for AJ sake. I had to be brave and block my childhood memories from weakening my resolve.

"Oh no! Sid, we are in the jungle. What will we do now? My parents will find us soon!" she said.

"Don't worry AJ, we will do something," I assured her, but I was frightened myself.

"No, we can't do anything! You just have to go without me or else they will kill you."

"They will kill me no matter what, and I can't leave you here all alone. I love you AJ," I said.

"But! But!"

"AJ, it is fate brought us together and now it will keep us together." I said, "Let's go AJ, we have to move now from here or else your parents will find us."

I started walking again. AJ was beside me, I could feel that. A strong cold wind was blowing from the south. And the sky above me was covered with dark grey clouds. I could easily hear the different sounds that the animals were making. Suddenly, something big and dark obstructed my path, putting me into shock. It was a snake! But luckily it went away without hurting me.

We were walking and walking with a hope of finding some help. I was tired, and my body was in deep pain due to the injuries from the accident and the painkillers had started to wear off now. I wanted to take rest for some time, but I couldn't because of AJ's parents.

"Sid, take some rest."

"No, I can't take rest and your parents can also catch up on us if we stopped."

"But you are in pain!" she urged.

"How do you know?" I asked politely.

"It's clearly visible on your face." She was worried.

"Don't worry about me," I urged.

"Sorry, Sid," AJ said, emotionally.

"Sorry for what?"

"Because of me, you are in so much trouble."

"No! Don't feel sorry. It's not your fault. This all is happening because of your evil parents."

"You are right Sid, but still if I didn't meet you, you would not have had to deal with all this.

"Don't say that. The day I met you was the best day of my life. So please don't say that ever again, because it hurts me."

"Okay, I will not," she assured.

From afar, I saw a small light glowing ahead of us. It gave me a glimmer of hope. Perhaps we could get some help now.

"Look AJ, a small light is glowing."

"Where?"

"Look straight," I indicated.

"Oh, yes!"

"Let's go towards it. May be we can find someone who could help us," I said. hopeful.

We headed towards it with a hope of finding someone who could help us. As we got closer, I saw a small, old and dilapidated hut which was made of bricks. It turned out that the small light was coming for a lantern hung inside the hut. The hut's door was open. We ventured inside the hut cautiously, but nobody was there. There was a small single wooden bed inside the hut placed at a corner. Next to the bed, stood a two-drawer wooden stand. There were lots of small empty glass bottles lying on the shelf. The old sofa near the window was in a bad shape. The hut was peppered with lots of weird stuff lying on the floor and elsewhere.

"Hello? Is anybody here? I am lost. Can you help please? Hello?" Suddenly, I heard a male voice.

"Who are you? And how did you get in?" He said in an angry voice.

When I looked towards the voice, I saw a middle-aged man of average built and average height standing with his arms folded across his chest. His hair was partially white and there was a big black mole near his lower lip which was very prominent. He had a shiny white goatee on his chin. He was dressed in all black—wearing black jeans and a black shirt.

"Sir, I am Sid. Please help me. I am lost in this jungle. Can you please tell me the way out?" I requested, a little wary of this strange man.

He was looking at me surprised. I felt as though he was observing something about me. After a long pause, he said, "Okay, I will help you. . . But First, tell me who is she?" He pointed towards AJ.

I was shocked. *How could he see AJ! Was he also dead? Was he a ghost?*

"How can he see me, Sid?" AJ muttered under her breathe.

"I don't know," I said whispered.

"You know, I can also *hear* you," the man said.

"But how can you see her? She is . . . dead." I said.

"I know she is dead."

"But how? Are you dead as well?" I asked scared.

"No, I am not dead! I am an . . . "

"Yes?" I egged him on.

"I am an Occultist," he replied.

"What? An occultist?" I inquired, dreading.

"Yes, an occultist. My name is Tony Blake, but you can call me Mr. Blake."

Despite how strange this man was, I decided to give him the benefit of doubt since our situation was dire.

"Mr. Blake, can you please help us?" I requested.

"Alright, I will, but first you have to tell me the whole story, so I can figure out how to help you," he insisted.

"Yes, sure," I replied.

I told him about AJ and her parents, how they used to torture her, about their accident and how they all died in a car accident.

"They are shameless and cruel people, how can they treat their own daughter like this!" he replied with a bewildered expression on his face; but anyway, what do they want from you now?" he questioned.

"They want to torture her further by killing me because she loves me," I replied. They don't want her to go from earth peacefully."

"Horrible people! Don't worry, you two! I will help you," Mr. Blake replied with certainty.

Chapter 13
Tony Blake

"*C*an I ask you something, Mr. Blake?"

"Yes, of course."

"You look like an Indian. So, why is your name Tony Blake?"

"Actually, I am half-Indian half-British. My mom was an Indian, and Dad was British. It was my father who named me," he explained.

Mr. Blake seemed like a nice and genuine person. He seemed eager to help us, but I was suspicious. I let my mind wander. *How will he help us? What if something went wrong? What if he has any ulterior motive? What if he is part of yet another ploy by AJ's parents.* All those questions were bothering me. I did not want anything to go wrong.

"What happened, Sid? What are you thinking? You seem tensed," AJ asked. She sounded worried.

"Nothing, AJ. Don't worry, I am fine," I lied.

Mr. Blake was looking at me. "Mr. Blake, how will you help us?" I inquired.

"I have studied occultism all my life. I have tamed many evil spirits. AJ's parents seem to be particularly evil since they continue to torture AJ even after her death! I can perform some magic and rituals to control them. First, I will have to call or lure them here and then I will capture them in a bottle so that they can never hurt you people again," he explained.

"Oh, can you really do that? That's a great idea! But what if the idea fails? What will we do then?" I asked.

Mr. Blake was listening to me patiently.

"Trust me, Sid, I have captured many evil spirits before. Look at the shelf behind you." He pointed towards the shelf. I looked toward the wooden shelf at the line of empty bottle stacked there. "Can you see those bottles?" he asked.

"Yes," I replied looking at the shelf which I had noticed before.

"These bottles are not empty. There are evil spirits inside those bottles which I have captured before." Mr. Blake picked up a bottle and showed it to me and AJ.

"Really?" My jaw dropped.

"Yes, nothing will go wrong, trust me," he assured us.

"I trust you, Mr. Blake."

"That's good." He had a bizarre smile on his face.

"One more thing, AJ told me that a Blue Light came to take her. So, why didn't it take them?" I questioned.

"They are evil spirits, Sid, the Blue Light will not take them as it is for good souls only. However, there is a red light which is solely for bad spirits," Mr. Blake explained.

"Oh, so why didn't the red light take them away?"

"I believe they died before their time. People who die before their time, their souls stay on earth till their time comes," he explained.

"Oh! So, will they stay here forever?" I asked curiously.

"No, someday they also will have to go from here but until then . . . I will capture these evil spirits in a bottle for you," he explained.

"Let's do it then," I said, excited.

"No, we can't do it right now. We have to wait until midnight," he replied.

I looked at my wristwatch. It was 6.30 in the morning. I got tensed because I needed to go back to the hospital now or else my parents would get to know that I am not in the hospital and they will start looking for me.

"What happened, Sid?" AJ asked.

"I have to go to the hospital, AJ," I replied in a distressed.

"Please! Don't go, Sid, what if my parents are still outside. They will kill you. You must stay," she requested, scared.

Mr. Blake was standing near the sofa. He was listening to our conversation. AJ was scared to let me go. I also wanted to stay with her, but I could not. I had to go to the hospital before my parents woke up. I saw Mr. Blake coming towards us.

He said, "Don't worry AJ; they can't do anything until sunset so you two are safe. Let him go."

"Really? See, AJ, are you happy now? Can I go?" I asked for her permission.

"Yes, if it's safe, and if you must go, then I understand," she replied in a gloomy tone.

"Oh, AJ, don't be sad, I will come as soon as possible," I promised.

"Don't worry Sid, you go. I will take care of her but don't forget to come before sunset, or else they will catch you," Mr. Blake said in a grim and serious tone.

"Bye, AJ," I said.

I left that place with a heavy heart. I came onto the main road after crossing through the jungle. I saw a cab coming through the distance. I stopped the cab and sat inside. The driver dropped me at the hospital gate. I rushed inside the gate. Fortunately, the guard was not at the gate. As I reached the corridor, I saw my parents were still sleeping. I breathed a sigh of relief and I straight away went to my room. I wore the hospital clothes again and hid the clothes I was wearing in a drawer.

I took out some painkillers from the drawer and poured a glass of water for myself. After taking the painkillers, I lay down on the bed. I tried to get some sleep, but I could not sleep much due to the intense pain. The physical exertion in the jungle had made the pain worse. But it was all worth in the end. I was ready to take any amount of pain for AJ.

Chapter 14
The Sunset

$\mathcal{I}$ was lying restless on my hospital bed. I heard the clock tick away the time. I gazed at the clock on the wall. It was 7.45 a.m. My mom entered the room with fresh clothes for me.

"Good morning, son," Mom said.

"Good morning," I replied.

"How are you feeling now?" she asked, concerned.

"I still have pain in my body," I told her.

"Don't worry, I will give you an injection for the pain. It seems like you didn't sleep at all last night."

"No Mom, I slept for some time. But I woke up at 4 o' clock in the morning due to the pain," I lied.

My mom gave me something to eat before giving me the medicine and the injection. After the injection, I fell asleep for some time. I woke at 2 o' clock in the afternoon. My mom was sitting on a chair lying next to me. And my dad was sitting on the sofa placed near the window.

"Mom," I called out to her.

"Yes, Sid. How are you feeling now?" she was still worried.

"I am fine now, Mom. Don't worry about me," I urged.

My father stood up and came near my bed. I have good news for you, my boy."

"What? Dad," I asked, curiously.

"Sid, you can change your clothes. You are discharged now! Let's go back home," Dad said merrily.

"Oh, that's great Mom," I replied.

I changed my clothes. I wore blue jeans with a black hoody. My driver was waiting for me at the entrance gate of the hospital. Mom opened the car door for me. Mom and I sat inside the car. Dad had some work at the hospital, so he stayed back there. As we reached home, Rita opened the door for us. She was looking genuinely pleased to see me back home.

"Welcome home. How are you?" Rita asked, politely.

"Thanks, Rita. I am fine now."

"Go to your room, Sid. Take some rest," Mom said.

"Okay, Mom."

"Rita, please make a vegetable soup and a healthy salad for Sid," Mom instructed.

I went to my room. I was hungry and tensed. I sat on my sofa and looked out of the window, it was raining. My mom entered the room with a bowl of soup and a salad. She kissed me on the forehead and sat next to me. When I was eating my meal, she was just looking at me lovingly. She looked cute, like a small baby.

"What happened, Mom? Why are you staring me like that?" I asked.

"Nothing, I just love watching you eat," she replied. "You look very cute. I feel happy that you are eating something healthy."

"Aww . . . Mom, I love you," I went and hugged her.

"I love you too, son," she replied, patting my back softly.

"Sid, I am going downstairs. You just take some rest. I will make your favourite dinner today," she said, merrily.

"Thanks, Mom," I replied.

Mom left the room leaving me alone with my thoughts. I was thinking about AJ's parents, how horrible they were, and thanking God at the same time for giving me such lovely and caring parents. I was feeling very sleepy and groggy due to all the medicines and injection. I decided to get some sleep and dozed off for two hours.

When I woke up, I went downstairs, and saw my mom. She was in the kitchen with Rita. She was making some healthy evening snack for me.

"Mom," I called.

"Oh, you woke up!"

I had to go to AJ on time, but I didn't know how to tell that to my mom. I was thinking of some excuse. After giving instructions to Rita for dinner, Mom sat next to me. She gave me the plate of the healthy snacks she had made for me.

"Mom, I have to go somewhere," I told her.

"Where?" she demanded.

"To my friend's house and I will also stay there tonight," I lied feigning confidence.

"No, Sid! You can't go. You are still recovering," she said, politely but firmly.

"Mom, please," I urged.

"No means No, Sid. I can't let you go. Please understand, son. You are not well," This time her voice even firmer.

"Okay, Mom, I understand. I won't go. Fine. Don't worry," I lied again.

Thankfully she didn't catch that I was lying this time. I ate the snacks which my mom had made for me. I gazed at the clock. It was 5 o' clock in the evening. I still had two hours to reach Mr. Blake's hut in the middle of the jungle before sunset. I stood up from my seat and started walking towards my room.

"Where are you going, Sid," Mom asked with a raised eyebrow.

"I am feeling sleepy, Mom. I am going to my room," I pretended to be very tired and made a sad face.

"Okay, okay. Take rest," she replied, falling for it.

I rushed to my room, locked my room from inside so that no one could come inside. Then, I changed my clothes, sat on the sofa, and after fifteen minutes, I took my phone and started typing the following message:

Mom, I have a little pain in my body, so I am taking the painkillers. Please don't wake me up for dinner or anything else. I love you. I texted this to her. A second later my phone buzzed with her reply. *Okay, Sid. Love you, too.*

I took a small blue bag and I put some painkillers and a small bottle of water in it. I could not go out from the front door because of my mother. The only way out, I thought, was jumping out of my room's window.

I opened the window and looked out, luckily, nobody was there. I was about to jump when suddenly, I saw my father's car coming in through the driveway. I quickly closed the window and stepped away.

After two minutes, I peeped out from the closed window. I saw my father going inside the house with his briefcase. I swiftly opened window again and stepped onto it and counted to three and just jumped! I tried to jump onto the garden patch, on the soft grass below me. Because of the clumsy jump, I injured my leg as I fell, I was not able to walk fast because of the injury.

I looked at my wristwatch. I still had half an hour to reach the Jungle before sunset. I was looking for the cab, but I couldn't find one. I was walking slowly and noticed it was beginning to get dark. The streetlights as usual were not working and I was becoming tensed. I saw the sun was also setting. It was happening a little before time. I was scared. And then, I heard a voice.

"Hello, Sid," someone called me from behind.

I stopped dead in my tracks.

Chapter 15
Magical Drops

$\mathcal{I}$ heard my name called many times, but I didn't look back. I was petrified, and my heart was pounding very fast. I felt like it would fall out of my chest. I was trying to walk as fast as I could, but I was not able to run because of my leg injury. I tripped over a stone and was about to fall but I somehow saved myself.

"Sid! Sid! Sid!"

Once again, I heard my name, this time more clearly. I said to myself, *'Don't be a coward. Turn around.* I gathered all my courage and looked back. "Oh! It's you, Mr. Blake!" I said breathing a sigh of relief.

"We were waiting for you. What took you so long?" he asked. He seemed genuinely worried.

"Sorry, my Mom didn't let me go and I got my leg injured. Then, I didn't get any cab," I explained.

"How did you get your injured again?"

"I jumped out of the window of my house. It's a long story. I will explain it to you later."

"Okay, let's go now, AJ is alone and worried," he replied.

"Let's go, but I can't walk fast," I said in a feeble voice.

"Don't worry, l brought my car," he informed. I was relieved.

We both sat inside the car, I had sweat all over my face. And due to brisk walking, my mouth and throat were dry. Mr. Blake gave me some water and a tissue. I wiped off my sweat and drank some water. The white car in which I sat was old and tatty. The brown leather seat covers of the car were torn from the edges. The foul smell of the car filled my nostrils.

Mr. Blake started the engine of the car; the engine made a roaring noise and we left for his hut. Although the car was in poor condition, I still felt warm and comfortable inside. It was better than walking with my new injury. Due to the fog, we were not able to look ahead on the road clearly.

"Sid, I have made something for you," Mr. Blake said, while taking out something from his pocket.

He gave me a small black bottle filled with greenish water of some sort. He instructed me to put it in my eyes.

"What *is* this?" I demanded.

"These are magical eye-drops," he replied.

"Magical eye-drops!" I asked. I was amazed.

"Yes, if you put these in your eyes, you will be able to see all supernatural things and ghosts," he explained.

"Really, so you are saying I would be able to see AJ?" I inquired.

"Yes, you would be able to see her," he replied while shifting the gear on the car.

I hugged him and put those drops in my eyes instantly. In the beginning my eyes started burning, but after a few seconds, the burning stopped. I was very happy. We were on our way. I was thinking of the moment when I would lay my eyes on AJ!

Suddenly, I saw someone standing in the middle of the road! As we got closer, I saw two middle-aged people a male and a female. They were trying to stop us, but Mr. Blake didn't stop the car, and drove right through them. Suddenly the fog engulfed the street lights and, I was not able to see anything clearly.

"What are you doing Mr. Blake? You hit those people!" I yelled.

"They were ghosts, Sid. I think they were AJ's parents."

"What are you saying!" I was dumbfounded.

"Look back, Sid, they are fine, and in fact they are following us," he said.

"Oh, no! What are we going to do now?" I asked, scared.

"Don't worry; they can't do anything, we are safe."

"Are you sure?" I said.

"Here, wear this." Mr. Blake gave me a shining silver bracelet.

"What's this?"

"I have done some magic on this to keep them away from us. This bracelet will keep you safe from them," he explained. I wore the bracelet on my right arm promptly. It fitted me perfectly.

When we reached the hut, Mr. Blake told me to go inside. I heard a loud creak when I opened the car gate. I was in a hurry, so I did not bother. The hut's door was open. As I ventured inside into the room, I saw AJ. I could finally see her! She was standing silently in the corner looking out of the window. I could see her thanks to Mr. Blake's magical eye drops. I walked towards her.

"Hey AJ," I said, merrily.

"Hey," she replied while turning towards me. Her eyes were sparkling.

"You are looking beautiful."

"What? Can you see me?" she asked, surprised.

"Yes, AJ!"

"How?" she demanded.

"Mr. Blake gave me some magical eye drops," I showed AJ the small bottle. I am so pleased that I can see you," I was beaming with happiness.

"How are you now, Sid," AJ asked, worriedly.

"I am fine."

"But you don't look fine."

"AJ, trust me, I am much better," I urged.

AJ and I were looking into each other eyes. I wanted to hold her in my arms and give her a kiss but I could not touch her.

Mr. Blake entered the room with some very weird stuff. He was holding a skull in his hand and bottles filled with some potions. He placed everything on the center table.

"What is this?" I demanded while walking towards him and all the stuff he placed on the table.

"This is the magical equipment that I will use to perform magic to capture and imprison AJ's parents in a bottle,"

"Oh," I muttered.

"Now, don't waste time, we have two hours to do this," Mr. Blake warned.

"What are you going to do? Can you please explain first?" I demanded.

"I am going to do some magic, which will force them to come here and when they come, I will capture them in an empty glass bottle, but this process can be very dangerous and requires a lot of mental and emotional strength from the participants. Especially from you, AJ," Mr. Blake said, in a grave tone.

As I glanced at AJ, she looked confused and scared, just like me.

Chapter 16
The Ouija Board

"I don't understand. Please, could you explain more clearly? They will not harm AJ, right?" I asked, concerned.

"Let me tell you. When I do the spell to call the spirits of AJ's parents here, they will struggle a lot before being imprisoned in the bottle. To save themselves, they will try everything they can to influence AJ's will. They will plead to her to get themselves free. They will emotionally blackmail her," he explained.

"Even so, she knows their reality; they will not be able to manipulate her," I said with confidence.

"No, Sid. It's a very powerful spell and it will be extremely painful for them. They will feel like they are burning alive. They will do anything to free themselves from this trap. Besides, this spell has a side-effect also," he informed.

"What side-effects?" I inquired.

"Although it will be very painful for them, it also inversely gives them the special power to hypnotize people in that short duration. So, they can hypnotize AJ and force her to do what they want," he explained.

"Oh, no! Can we do something to control them then?" I asked.

"No, but AJ, you have to be strong. You shouldn't fall into their trap. I will not be able to do anything at that moment to help you. So, stay strong. One more important thing . . . you shouldn't look at them directly in their eyes," he replied.

"Okay, I will remember that," she said in a low tone.

AJ and I were standing in the drawing room of that small hut in the middle of the jungle and looking at Mr. Blake. The weather outside was fear-inducing. I could hear the heavy thunderstorm raging outside. Mr. Blake opened a drawer and took out a black bag. He opened his bag and took out a huge crystal ball from inside. It was very dark in the hut now, and I was not able to see anything. Mr. Blake had turned off the lights and instead lighted lots of candles all around the room. After lighting the room with candles, he sat comfortably on the floor cross-legged, with the crystal ball in his hands. He closed his eyes for some time and seemed to be meditating.

After some time, he gazed inside the crystal ball. After about five minutes, he placed the crystal ball on the wooden stand placed in front of him. When we gazed at the ball, we noticed a mist was forming slowly. Suddenly, we saw two people in that crystal ball. It was none other than AJ's parents!

"Look! There they are!" Mr. Blake showed them to us. My skin crawled, and my body was pumping with adrenaline.

"They are somewhere in the jungle," Mr. Blake said, and placed an old skull in front of us and instructed us to sit on the floor as well. We sat down on the carpet in front of him. He took out an odd-looking wooden flat board marked with letters of the English alphabet and the numbers 0-9, and the words yes or no, along with various symbols which I did not understand.

Mr. Blake threw a black powder on AJ, suddenly. AJ and I were stunned.

"Mr. Blake! Why did you throw this on AJ?"

"This is a magical powder. It will give AJ a special power."

"What type of power?"

"She will able to touch things temporally." Then, he told AJ to place her finger on that board.

"What is this?" I demanded.

"It's an Ouija board. It will help us to call them here. AJ, don't pull your finger off from this board no matter what or else all this will be in vain," he replied.

"Okay, " she said, tensed.

AJ placed her middle finger on the board and when the clock struck twelve, Mr. Blake started the process. He began reciting spells again and again.

"Hear me, you horrible spirits!

Come to me from the other side.

Remove the chain from time and space. I call upon you now."

I was sitting next to AJ with my finger on the board as well. She was nervous and scared; I could see the tension on her face. I consoled her and cupped her hand in my hand. The feeling I felt by touching her was incredible. Suddenly, we saw some flashes of light in front of us. Mr. Blake told us to ignore it. He continued reciting the spells.

"Hear me you, horrible spirits.

Come to me from the other side.

Remove the chain from time and space. I call upon you now."

The spell was very powerful. I could feel that. All the candles were suddenly extinguished. The atmosphere inside became very grave and frightening. We were in the middle of the process of calling AJ's parents. Suddenly, AJ pulled her finger off the board! Mr. Blake and I exchanged a quick worried glance.

"What have you done?" Mr. Blake shouted at AJ.

"Sorry, Mr. Blake. I don't know what happened!"

"Mr. Blake, she is nervous. It's not easy for her," I defended her.

"I understand that, but she should not have done that."

"Can we do something now?" I asked.

"Let me try one more time."

Mr. Blake started reciting the spells again, more aggressively now. AJ placed her finger once again on that board. Mr. Blake started reciting the spells again.

"Hear me you, horrible spirits.

Come to me from the other side.

Remove the chain from time and space, I call upon you now."

Suddenly, it became dark inside the room, and the whole room was covered with a kind of mist, I was not able to see anything. We heard someone calling AJ's name. We became very scared, but Mr. Blake continued the process.

"AJ! AJ!" someone called her again.

"Don't pay any attention AJ; they are here," Mr. Blake said.

"Who?" I asked.

"AJ's parents," he said.

"I can't see them because of this mist," I explained. My heart was beating fast. AJ hold my hand tightly.

"You will, in a couple of minutes," he said, "AJ, stay strong. Don't pull off your finger from the board at any cost," he requested.

Chapter 17

Capturing the Spirits

*A*fter some time, the smoke cleared away. I could see the room clearly. I saw AJ's parents standing outside the door of the hut! They looked astonished and confused.

"Mr. Blake . . . they are here!" I informed, pointing at the door.

"I know, Sid, and in no time, they will be captured in a bottle," he said confidently.

I looked at AJ. She seemed stressed. She was nervous, and her body was shaking. I tried to calm her, but that did not work. Suddenly, her parents came a little closer to us. They began to plead to us to set them free. They were crying, but I could feel that those tears were fake. They were trying to manipulate her just as Mr. Blake had told us earlier.

"Don't say a single word. I know you people all too well," AJ said to her parents in a strong voice.

"AJ, we are your parents. We know that we treated you awfully but please don't do this to us. This is very painful." They begged.

"Don't listen to them AJ, just concentrate here," Mr. Blake said.

They were continuously pleading us all to set them free, but we stayed strong. The atmosphere inside the room was becoming scarier. Mr. Blake was still chanting the spells:

"Oh lord! Oh lord!By earth and air,
By water and fire,
Please help me to capture these horrible spirits."

"AJ, your brother loved you. He will never want you to do this to us," they said.

"No, he was a good human being. He always supported me. He knew you people were evil," AJ said. "He always helped me."

"Look at us, please. At least, look at us," they said, with tears flowing down their cheeks.

"AJ, don't look at them," I said. I was worried. AJ's heart seemed to be melting somewhat.

"Don't worry, Sid, I will not," she managed to say. Although she said she would not look at them, I was not convinced. She seemed to be acting strange and seemed to be struggling internally.

"My brother . . . my little brother . . . He would not want me to hurt our parents . . ." she seemed to be talking to herself. "No! No! They are evil! They are trying to manipulate me!" she said in the next moment.

Meanwhile, Mr. Blake put his hand in a black plastic bag. He took out a box from the bag and opened it. Inside the box was a white powder. He took a handful of the powder and threw that powder on AJ's parents. They started panicking as soon as it hit them. I could feel that it was quite painful for them. There face turned pale and eyes become bloodshot.

"Please! Stop this! This powder is burning us," they screamed in pain.

"Mr. Blake, can you do something else that is less painful?" AJ asked. "I can't see them in pain."

AJ had tears in her eyes. She was shaking. Mr. Blake took out a bottle from his bag. He once again threw the powder on them.

"AJ, don't do this to yourself; they deserve this. Please don't cry for them," I tried to give her some confidence.

"I know, but I can't see them in pain. They are my parents," she replied.

"AJ, you are a pure soul, and they made your life a living hell, even then you are thinking about them?"

AJ's parents were still trying to get themselves out of the situation. They promised that if we leave them, they will never hurt us and will leave AJ and me alone.

"Shut up, you two! We don't trust you," I yelled.

I saw AJ. She was getting weaker and weaker, I could feel. Her hands were shaking, and she was crying. She told me she could not do this to them no matter what they did to her. She was giving up. She was slowly turning her face towards them, but I stopped her.

"AJ, look at me! They are influencing you! Don't listen to them, just look at me, and this will all end soon," I assured. I wiped her tears gently.

Mr. Blake commanded me to open the empty bottle lying in front of me. I opened the bottle and handed over to him. He again threw that powder on them and started chanting the spell loudly.

"Oh lord! Oh lord! By earth and air,
By water and fire,
Please help me to capture these horrible spirits.
I cast the spell now."

AJ's parents were shouting in pain. The whole room was filled with their screams. Mr. Blake held the bottle in his right hand, and from the left hand, he threw the powder for one last time.

Soon the shouting ceased, and I saw Mr. Blake was doing some strange movements with his hands. Suddenly, AJ's parents turned into a puff of smoke, and Mr. Blake captured that whirling smoke in the bottle and closed the bottle tightly.

He stood up and placed that bottle on the shelf with the other bottles. AJ's eyes were closed tightly.

"AJ, open your eyes! It's done! They are gone forever," Mr. Blake, said merrily.

"Oh! Thank God," I said. I thanked Mr. Blake for helping us profusely. When I turned back, I saw AJ was standing near the window. She was still crying and shaking. I talked to her for some time and tried to calm her down.

"AJ, they are gone! Now we are free."

"Yes, we are. Thank you so much".

"You don't have to say thank you to me."

She turned towards Mr. Blake and thanked him as well.

She came towards me happily. I thought, finally, we were free from those evil spirits. Now I can spend whatever little time AJ had with her on earth, peacefully. Suddenly,

AJ's expression changed. She looked scared. Tears were rolling down on her face once again.

"What happened AJ?" I asked, bewildered.

"The Blue Light . . .The Blue Light has come," she said in a scared tone.

Chapter 18

The Body

"*W*here is it?" I asked, shocked.

"Behind you, Sid," she replied. Her eyes were wet.

I turned around, and I could see that light. The magical eye drops were still working. It was a very bright light. I had to squeeze my eyes a bit to look at it properly. It was coming closer and closer. I looked at AJ; she seemed disturbed. I had tears in my eyes as well.

"Mr. Blake, please do something," I requested.

"I can't do anything, Sid," he said in a weak voice.

Due to the presence of the Blue Light, the atmosphere of the room had changed. The blue flashes of light were all over the room. I could feel divine energy coming from the Blue Light. A lovely strong fragrance filled my nose. It was also coming from the Blue Light. The brightness of the light was hurting my eyes. Mr. Blake gave me a pair of special glasses to wear.

"Why are you giving me these glasses?"

"If you wear these your eyes will not get hurt. You will able to see the Blue Light clearly," he explained.

I wore the glasses swiftly. Mr. Blake was right. I could see the Blue Light clearly. I did not have to squint my eyes anymore. I saw a figure inside the Blue Light. It was wearing white clothes. It was tall and had golden hair. I could see its divine brown eyes vaguely. I could not tell whether it was a male or female figure. It was like a floating angel in white robes.

"AJ, your time is over. We must go," A strong firm voice emanated from the Blue Light.

AJ's face turned pale. She was in shock. Her whole body was shaking.

"No, don't do this, please. Don't take her away from me," I begged.

"Sorry Sid, I have to take her away from here," the Blue Light said.

AJ was crying and feeling helpless. She came towards me and extended her hand to touch me, but it went right across me. She tried it again but was unable to touch and hold me.

"Mr. Blake, why can't she touch me?"

"I think her special power has stopped working."

My heart stopped beating. Tears streamed down my cheeks. Mr. Blake was standing in the corner observing everything helplessly. AJ was standing in front of me. I was feeling terrible at that moment. The love of my life was going away from me forever, and I could not do anything. AJ turned away from me, but I tried to stop her. I tried to hold her hand, but my hand went right across.

"Let me go, Sid," she said in a low tone.

"No, I can't."

"Please, Sid. Let me go. I don't belong here anymore."

"No! No!" I felt like someone had stabbed straight through my heart.

"Good-bye Sid," she said while walking towards the Blue Light.

"No! No! I can't live without you," I pleaded.

"Sid, you have to live for your family. Please forget me and move on with your life."

"Take me with you as well," I requested the Blue Light. "I don't want to live my life without her."

"No, I can't do that," the Blue Light said.

"Why? Take me, please," I begged once again.

"Your time has not come yet."

"Don't worry, then. I will kill myself. Then you will have to take me with you," I said in a strong voice.

"Don't do that to yourself, Sid," AJ said crying. "Think about your parents. If you die, they will also die with you."

We both were crying and pleading. We were not ready to be separated. Mr. Blake was watching all this. He said that love like this was very rare. He also requested the Blue Light to not to take AJ with it.

"I know they love each other truly. I also want to leave her on earth, but I can't do it," the Blue Light said.

"But why?" Mr. Blake asked.

"It's not possible."

"Please think about it. AJ's parents never loved her. This boy can give her everything she ever dreamed of," Mr. Blake requested.

"I understand, but we can't go against nature."

"Please! Please," I requested and pleaded.

There was silence for a long time. All three of us exchanged glances. *Was the Blue Light considering our pleas? Would it let AJ live? Would AJ and I be reunited?*

"Alright. I will let AJ live. But to bring her back to life, I need her mortal body," he explained.

I could not believe my ears! He had agreed! He had agreed, finally! But we did not know anything about AJ's dead body. I looked at Mr. Blake expectantly and asked him if he could do something.

"I can help you to find her body," Mr. Blake assured.

He went outside the hut to search for something in his car. He took out a wooden box from inside his car.

"What is this?" A curious sensation overwhelmed me.

"Let's go inside, I will explain in front of all," he replied.

He took out a compass from the box. It was a golden vintage compass.

"It is a magical compass. It will help us in finding AJ's body," he explained to all of us.

He started chanting a spell.

"Oh! Lord oh! Lord,

please help me to find AJ's body,

Oh! Lord oh! Lord,

please help me to find AJ's body."

He chanted that spell for five minutes with his eyes closed.

After five minutes, he suddenly opened his eyes. He seemed pleased.

"Sid, I know where her body is," Mr. Blake announced.

"Where?" I asked merrily.

"I don't know the exact location but its buried somewhere in the jungle," he replied. "And luckily, her body has not decayed yet."

AJ and I became very happy. We looked at each other hopeful. I hugged Mr. Blake happily and thanked him for helping us again.

"Sid, let me warn you before you proceed. There will be some dire consequences that AJ will have to bear as a result of AJ's resurrection from the dead," the Blue Light warned.

AJ and I gazed at each other, tensed.

"What type of consequences?" I asked.

"You will get to know that in the future. It could go against AJ's interest or be in her favour. So, AJ, do you really want to live again?"

"Yes, I can bear anything to be with Sid. I love him immensely."

"Whatever may come, we will face it together," I assured AJ.

"Well then. As you wish."

"Mr. Blake, hurry up. We have to bring her body back here," I requested.

"Yes, do it fast. I can only give you two hours. If you don't come before that, I will take her away with me," the Blue Light said. "I will not be able to do anything then."

"No, that will not happen," I assured.

"Let's go, Mr. Blake."

"Give me one minute, Sid. I have to take my bag."

Mr. Blake picked up his bag. He also took out a torch from the middle-drawer of his cabinet.

Chapter 19

The Graveyard

$\mathcal{M}$r. Blake and I ventured out of the hut. It was very dark outside, and the weather was not pleasant.

"Sid," AJ called my name and came outside.

"Yes, AJ."

"Take care of yourself. Thank you for doing this for me."

"I am doing this for myself. So, you don't have to thank me."

"I am very lucky that I meet you, Sid."

"I am lucky too. Thank you for coming in my life. "

AJ was overcome with emotion. She also thanked Mr. Blake.

AJ went back inside, and Mr. Blake and I entered the forest. I could barely see anything. So, I turned on my phone's flashlight. We started walking. Mr. Blake was holding a compass in his right hand and a torch in his left hand.

"Mr. Blake, why are you holding that compass?" I asked. I was curious.

"Sid, I have magically linked this compass with AJ's body, now we just have to follow the directions shown on this compass," he explained.

"Okay, so in which direction should we go."

"South," he said while looking at the compass. I saw the needle of the compass moving slowly towards South.

We both headed in that direction. It was cold outside, and I was shivering. Luckily, Mr. Blake had a spare jacket in his bag. He took it out from the bag and gave it to me.

I wore the jacket swiftly. We continued our search, but we were not able to find anything. With every moment passing, I was becoming more and more restless. My heart beat kept increasing due to the rising tension.

One hour passed. "Mr. Blake, we have to hurry, we just have two hours in total remember?" I said, tensed.

"I know, Sid."

He stopped walking, suddenly. He once again looked at the compass. "Sid, now we have to move towards North," he told me.

"Are you sure this compass is showing us the right direction?" I asked. I was suspicious now.

"Yes, Sid. I am sure."

"Mr. Blake, is there any graveyard in this jungle?"

"Oh! Yes, there is. How can I forget?" he said.

"Should we check there?" I replied.

"Yes, you are right, let's go."

After fifteen minutes of walking, we reached the graveyard. It was a hundred-year-old graveyard. The long gates of the graveyard were closed. A strong foul odour filled my nose.

"Sid, open the gate," Mr. Blake ordered.

A gush of chilly wind blew bitterly making me shiver just as I opened the rusty ancient iron gates. The gates made a creaking sound as I opened them. The graveyard was very eerie. As we moved into the graveyard, a chill ran down my spine. There were hundreds of graves. The grass around them looked damp, and most of the flowers were dead.

We started looking for AJ's grave, but most of the graves did not have any names on it. I became tensed. I thought how will we ever find her grave?

"Mr. Blake, there are lots of graves here, how can we find AJ's?" I asked.

"Don't worry; my compass will help us."

He opened his compass once again. He started walking near the graves slowly; one by one, he was going near each grave and placing the compass on top of it. Suddenly, his compass started vibrating over one grave. The needles were moving swiftly in a circular motion.

"Here it is!" he said. "Sid, come quickly. We must dig this grave."

We did not have any tools to dig the grave. I was searching for something that could help us to dig. I went to the other side of the graveyard alone. I heard some strange whispers, but I did not bother much. I saw a shovel lying near a grave. I picked it up and went back to Mr. Blake. When I was going back, I heard dogs howling in the distance. I could also hear the eerie hooting of the owls.

"I found a shovel, Mr. Blake" I announced, merrily.

"Oh, that's great. Now start digging the grave," he prompted.

I started digging the grave with all my power. Suddenly, I hurt my hand as the shovel slipped slightly from my hand. Blood came oozing out from the injury. Mr. Blake took out a white hanky from his pocket and wrapped it around my hand tightly.

"Sid, give the shovel to me. I will dig the grave now."

I gave the shovel to Mr. Blake. He started digging the grave. There was a small hill of mud next to us now. The fresh and earthy smell of mud hit my nose. After fifteen minutes, we saw a coffin.

"Mr. Blake! Look! It is a coffin!" I pointed towards the coffin.

It was a plain and simple wooden coffin. Mr. Blake and I opened the coffin with some effort. There it was! I saw AJ's lifeless body! I was very disturbed and scared to see AJ's body lying in that manner, but I knew I must be brave and carry on because it was the only way she could live again. The mere thought of seeing AJ alive motivated me to go through this difficult ordeal. Tears were rolling down my face. I looked at Mr. Blake; he too seemed overcome with emotion. We took out AJ's body from the coffin and placed it on the ground.

"How will we take her body from here?" Mr. Blake asked.

"I will carry her in my arms."

"Sid, I don't think you will able to walk like this."

"I can do anything to see AJ alive," I replied.

Mr. Blake helped me carry AJ's dead body. I had a sharp pain throughout my body, but somehow, I coped with it. We stepped out of the graveyard with AJ's body in my arms.

"We only have forty-five minutes left. How we will reach there so soon?" I asked. I was worried and sweating.

"I know a shortcut," he said while putting the compass in his pocket.

"Why didn't we use this shortcut when we were coming here?" I said angrily.

"Sorry for that Sid!" he said.

"No need to say sorry, I was just pulling your leg!" We laughed. We finally reached our destination and entered the hut.

"We are back," I announced merrily.

I saw AJ was sitting near the door. She looked stressed. The Blue Light was nowhere to be seen. My heart filled with anxiety. Mr. Blake also became tensed. I thought we were late! Did it leave early? I shook my head in confusion and went towards AJ.

Chapter 20
One Last Time

"What happened, where is the Blue Light?" I asked AJ. I was fearful.

"I am here." The Blue Light appeared in front of us. I breathed a sigh of relief.

"I thought you were gone," I said.

"If I were gone, I would have taken AJ with me," the Blue Light said.

I placed AJ's body on the couch. The Blue Light came near the body. It called AJ near her body. It placed its hand on AJ's head. After about five minutes, I saw a light near AJ's soul. Suddenly, the light disappeared, and AJ's soul also vanished.

"Where is she?" I asked. My heart was beating out of my chest.

"Sid!" I heard my name. When I looked towards the couch, it was AJ who had called my name. I breathed a sigh of relief.

"She is alive now," the Blue Light said.

I was ecstatic! I felt like dancing! AJ seemed so happy! I hugged Mr. Blake.

"One minute, please," Mr. Blake said in a dramatic tone.

"Now, what happened?" I asked, worried.

"Everyone knows that AJ died, and now she is alive again. Everyone will start questioning you guys, what will you tell them?" Mr. Blake asked us.

"I already took away the memories of the people who knew about AJ's death, hereafter they will only remember that AJ's parents and brother had died, but Sid saved her," the Blue Light explained.

"Oh, thank you very much," I said merrily.

"It's no problem, but I have spared her life once. It will not happen again."

"There will be no need for that. I will take care of her. I will not let anything happen to her till my last breath," I assured.

We all thanked the Blue Light after that and within a second, it vanished. AJ was standing in front of me. I touched her and when I did that, I finally felt an indescribable peace. I cupped her face in my hands. Her eyes were sparkling with happy tears.

"AJ, you are alive," I said. My eyes filled with tears of happiness as well.

"I know," she said as if she unable to believe it herself.

She hugged me tightly and kissed me on my forehead. Finally, the love of my life was alive again. Mr. Blake was watching us silently. He looked genuinely pleased.

"Mr. Blake, thank you very much," I said while hugging him again.

"Yes, thank you very much. Because of you and Sid, I am alive again. I don't know how I will repay you both," AJ said.

"Just take care of yourself, AJ. I don't want anything else from you," Mr. Blake said.

Mr. Blake insisted that he will drop us at my house in his car. I held AJ's hand, and we went outside with Mr. Blake. All of us sat inside his car. AJ and I sat in the backseat of the car. The engine started quickly with a roaring sound. We were just ten minutes away from home. Suddenly, Mr. Blake's phone rang loudly. He answered his phone. It was his brother's phone. He was in the jungle at the hut and wanted to meet Mr. Blake. He was in a hurry. Mr. Blake told us that he was an occultist as well.

"Mr. Blake you can drop us here, it's fine," I suggested.

"Why?"

"My house is just ten minutes away. We can walk from here. You should go, Mr. Blake, your brother is waiting for you."

"Are you sure? Both of you seem tired."

"Yes, we are, but we will be fine."

"Alright, as you say. Just take care of yourself."

"You too take care of yourself."

We stepped outside the car, waved goodbye to Mr. Blake, and started walking towards home. Mr. Blake started the engine after saying goodbye to us, turned around and sped back towards the jungle. AJ and I held each other's hands and started walking.

AJ looked at me, romantically. I was on cloud nine. When we reached home, I saw my mom was standing outside the door. She was talking to someone on the phone.

"Oh! No, what will we do now? Your mom is standing outside," AJ muttered.

"How do you know she is my mom?"

"I saw her on our date that night, at your house."

"Oh! AJ, can you do something for me," I requested.

"Of course, I will."

"Listen, you just divert her attention by talking to her. Meanwhile, I will make my way to my bedroom," I explained.

"But what will I talk about?"

"Tell her that you are my friend from school and you heard about my accident. So, you have come to meet me," I explained to her.

"Okay, Sid. I can do that," she replied.

AJ went towards my mom. She started talking to her. I ventured into the house through the back door. Rita was in the kitchen. Fortunately, she did not see me. I swiftly went up to my room. I changed my clothes and hid my bag in the closet. I lay down on my bed quietly. After five minutes, there was a knock at the door.

Knock! Knock!

"Sid, are you awake?" Mom asked.

"Yes, Mom. Please, come in," I said, politely.

"Sid, a beautiful girl from your school has come to meet you," she replied.

AJ entered my room, smiling.

"Hey, Sid"

"Oh, AJ. Hey."

"How are you, Sid?"

"I am fine. Please have a seat."

Rita bought juice and some snacks for us. After serving us, she left the room. My mom was looking at me suspiciously.

"You never told me you had a girlfriend," Mom asked. She raised an eyebrow.

"I told you, Mom. But you didn't believe me!" I winked at AJ.

"No, you didn't," she protested.

"Yes. I did! Let me introduce her again! This is AJ, my invisible girlfriend!" I said laughing.

"What?" Mom said. She was completely stunned.

AJ and I could not help but laugh at her confusion.

www.ingramcontent.com/pod-product-compliance
Lightning Source LLC
Chambersburg PA
CBHW051514260626
47162CB00008B/2970